Lucky Chance

MARINE FOR YOU: BOOK ONE

MARISSA DOBSON

Dedication

To all the men and women in uniform, who stand up and fight for our country. Thank you for all you do. May your road always lead you back home to your loved ones.

To my readers. Each of you are amazing. Thank you for loving my stories as much as I do. I hope you enjoy Lucky's book and the upcoming *Marine for You* books. After all, you are the ones who have demanded them. I promise that Angelo and Sam will have their own books soon.

I also want to dedicate this book to my amazing team. My editors, Rosa Sophia and Molly Daniels. My beta readers and my proofers. Teresa and all the work she does for my street team and keeping me on track. You are all amazing.

Last, but not least, to my wonderful husband, Thomas. You're an amazing, supportive husband, and I couldn't do this without you. Thank you for watching Pup Cameron so I can write. One day, he will be mature and won't be such a handful.

Chapter One

With his long legs stretched out in front of him, Gunnery Sergeant Lucky Diamond sat in front of his Sergeant Major's desk, unable to believe what he had just heard. He tried to focus his attention on the stack of papers on the corner of the desk, and hide his disapproval from his Sergeant Major because that would only make things worse. If Sergeant Major Dillon Graves knew Lucky didn't want to do what was at hand, then he'd make damn sure there were more unpleasant duties in the future. Marines followed orders, no matter how nasty they might be.

"It's customary for you to say something once your Sergeant Major gives you orders, not just sit there like a damn bump on a log." Dillon clasped his hands on the desk before him and watched Lucky.

"Yes, Sergeant Major." He wasn't sure how he managed that without any sarcasm in his voice.

"You'll do it then?"

Lucky wanted to scream *hell no*, that he wasn't going to take part in a military cook-off no matter what it benefited, but his Sergeant Major would have the final say. It was best to keep his mouth closed until he knew what his orders were. "Are my orders to take part in this charity cook-off?"

"Yes." Dillon leaned back in his chair. "You're our best chance of winning."

"Isn't there something my time could be better spent on? A volunteer deployment? Crash test dummy? Target for shooting practice?"

Dillon raised an eyebrow in question. "I believe you're going to be more challenging than I thought. All the times you've cooked for the men, turning that shit into something edible, and now you won't go win this for our branch, for the money to go to wounded Marines. I thought better of you, Gunnery Sergeant Diamond."

Guilt. Just as his mother would have used and it worked every time. With a deep exhale, he nodded. "I'll do it."

Sergeant Major Graves hit the intercom button on his desk phone. "Send her in."

A second later, the door opened and in stepped a woman. Her heels clicked along the floor announcing her, but when she came to stand next to Lucky and he caught sight of her, his jaw nearly dropped. That long hair, the same reddish brown he remembered from high school, and her piercing green eyes, were engrained in his memory from their last encounter. "As I live and breathe…Madison North."

"You two know each other?" Dillon asked, looking between them.

"Yes." Madison nodded, her gaze still on Lucky. "It's been years…"

"More than a dozen years since high school." Lucky rose from the chair, and wanted to wrap his arms around her. It was like time had stopped. She was as beautiful as the last time he'd seen her. "What are you doing here?"

"She's here to get you ready for the competition. Test out your recipes on her, whatever you need to be ready. You have two weeks before the cook-off," Dillon explained.

"Sergeant Major, the platoon has a training session the day after tomorrow. There isn't time—"

Dillon held up his hand, stopping Lucky before he could continue. "You need to focus on winning this for your fellow Marines, so I've approved you for leave until after the competition. Now, you better be on your way. I believe Ms. North has already made plane reservations for this evening."

"Reservations? Where are we going?"

"I had a car drop me off from the airport, so if you don't mind driving, I can explain on the way." She ran her hand over the thick leather planner in her hands. "Sergeant Major Graves, I'll make sure he does his best."

"I have no doubt about him." Dillon turned back to the paperwork on his desk, clearly dismissing them.

"My truck is just outside in the parking lot." Lucky held open the door of the office for her before shutting it behind them. "It's been too long. What have you been doing all these years?"

"After college, I was offered a job in New York, with a public relations firm. Two months ago, I was hired by the government to bring some good publicity to the military to offset the war. A promotional campaign to show the men and women in uniform in a better light."

"So, I can blame this cook-off on you, then?" He led her through the building toward the parking lot and his truck, all the time wondering how he had managed to get caught up in the whole situation. Out of all the Marines, how had *he* been the one they chose, and why?

"Actually, that was my boss. Her son did a barbecue competition a few months ago, and she thought, why not? It would be good promotion, and there could be a prize for different military charities. So, here we are."

"No, actually, here we are." He nodded to his silver pick-up truck. "What time is the flight, and where are we going?"

She stopped by the tailgate and looked at her watch before continuing around to the passenger side. "Oh, you have loads of time, we don't have to be at the airport until seven, and we're going to Denver. That's where the cook-off will be held."

He followed her lead, and got into the truck before starting the engine. He glanced at her. "Seven this evening? That's only a few hours." He checked his mirrors, making sure he was clear before dashing across both lanes for the exit he needed.

"Where are we going?"

"If I'm leaving town for two weeks, I need to stop by Ace and Gwen's house." He glanced over at her. "I bet you didn't hear he married almost a year ago, and now they have a child named Roulette."

She remembered the wedding invitation that she'd shoved on top of the refrigerator. Out of sight, out of mind. "Is he still a Navy SEAL?"

"Could you really see him giving it up?" He laughed at the thought. Ace was as dedicated to the SEALs as Lucky was to the Marines.

She shook her head. "No, it's what he always wanted to do. What about Wynn? How's she?" Another wedding invite that had been stored away to forget about, but she couldn't help but wonder about his little sister.

"She married Boom, a SEAL on Ace's squad, and she's about to have a baby girl any day now. Besides that, she's busy with Roll of the Diamond, her women's boutique, and Love of a Diamond, a baby boutique. She doesn't run the day-to-day operation for the stores but she does all their designs."

"I saw a few of her things in a shop on Fifth Avenue in New York City. I couldn't believe it. She was also in New York at the beginning of the year. I wanted to meet up with her, but I was out of town on business." She stared out the window, adding, "I'll say one thing for the Diamond crew, you were always go-getters. You knew what you wanted and went for it. Nothing would stand in your way."

"Sometimes there's a cost to that determination." He knew the sadness leaked through in his voice, but there was no way to banish it. He had lost a lot because of his commitment to the Marines.

"There's that as well." She nodded. "If you want to visit with your family before you leave, you could just drop me off at a café and pick me up whenever you're ready."

"No." He glared over at her. "I won't have that. Plus, we only need to stop in for a few minutes, to let them know I'll be out of town. They'll make sure to pick up my mail for me. Then we can head over to my condo so I can pack. Afterward, maybe dinner before heading to the airport. What do you say?"

He knew asking her to dinner sounded like they were picking back up where they had left off, but if they were going to be forced together for the next two weeks, they had to at least have a civil time together. After all, he wasn't interested in getting involved with someone. He enjoyed the freedom of his life, seeing whomever he wanted, coming and going as he pleased.

"Why not? We'll be spending a lot of time together over the next two weeks, so we might as well catch up over dinner before we fly out." She nodded and slid her hand over her planner.

That had been a nervous gesture in school, and he wasn't surprised it was still there. He only wondered what had her so worked up. "Everything okay?"

"Fine." She did it again, clearly lying to him.

"You always used to rub your hand along the curve of your books in school." When he caught her looking at him, he smiled. "You're doing it now, with the planner."

"I didn't know until I arrived who was chosen to represent the Marines for the competition; otherwise I'd have taken one of the other branches."

"Why?" Coming to a stop at a red light, he looked over at her.

"After the way things ended with us…" She didn't seem able to finish her thought, or even meet his gaze any longer.

"They didn't end *that* bad. We just decided it would be too hard for us to continue seeing each other." A horn blared from behind him, forcing his attention back to the road and the now green light. "You were going off to college and me to boot camp. It would have been difficult with the distance. I thought it was a mutual decision, and that we'd stay friends. Sure, we lost touch over the years, but a lot of people do. They get so wrapped up in their own lives they forget about the people they care about. What I don't understand is why you would avoid coming back and working with me if you knew I was the Marine?"

"Sometimes it's best to leave the past where it is. There is no reason our history should be dragged into the present. We'll get through this, you'll win the competition, and we'll go our separate ways. It's as simple as that."

There was a lingering doubt within him that warned him it wouldn't be that simple. Fate had brought them together again. It was as if all the years they had been apart melted away, leaving only the longing for what they once had. She was the first woman he'd made love to, the one woman no other could hold a candle to. He never stopped loving Madison, but it had been her idea to dissolve their relationship—as she had kindly put it so many years ago.

Madison sat in the passenger seat of Lucky's truck clutching her planner as the town she grew up in sped past. She hadn't been back to her hometown since she left for college. During her sophomore year in college, her parents had decided to leave Virginia Beach and move closer to her father's family in Florida. After they left, there seemed to be no reason to come back here, even though it was the one place she had always considered home. Florida never felt like home to her. She didn't even have a room to stay in when she visited her parents.

It wasn't so much her family's move that had kept her away; it was the memories of her time with Lucky and the rest of the Diamond crew. Everywhere she looked, she saw ghosts of yesteryear. The pizza parlor in which she, Lucky, Ace, Gwen, and Wynn had spent so much time. Or the movie cinema where she and Lucky had their first date. She wished she could run in the opposite direction. This wasn't the time to take a trip down memory lane, not with the secret that was growing within her.

"I'm sure Gwen and Wynn would love to see you before we left town. Or even when we come back. It's been too long."

Her thoughts flashed from memories of him to those of her two best friends. Through the years, she had kept in touch with them, mostly exchanging Christmas and birthday cards, a phone call here or there. Even though she had received wedding invitations from both of them, she hadn't come back to town for them. Like with Lucky, the doors to those friendships had closed. They were in the past and even though it sent a pain through her heart, that's where they needed to stay.

"Did you hear me?"

"We don't have time." She tried to reason without having to reveal why she didn't want to deal with a reunion.

"Then, when we get back."

"I won't be coming back to Virginia. On our return trip, we'll part ways in Washington D.C. and you'll return here to your normal duties." It might have sounded harsh, but that's what the future held for them. Two weeks, then she could put him back in the past and keep her feelings for him stuffed away.

"They'll be disappointed that they didn't get to see you." He paused at the stop sign before turning right and heading out of town toward Ace's house.

She remembered hearing that Ace had bought the family home when his parents wanted to downsize and travel. Another place that held too many memories, but she had no plans to get out of the truck. Since her offer to wait at a café in town didn't work, she'd wait in the truck and let him handle his business.

They rode in silence, and her thoughts continued to travel into the past. "Only a few hours…"

"What's that?" He shot her a sideways glance as he kept his attention on the road before him.

She hadn't meant to say it aloud, only in her thoughts. "Oh, nothing."

"You're anxious to get out of town. Aren't you?" When she said nothing, he added, "You keep looking at your watch, and I'd guess you're counting the hours until we're on the plane to Denver. Is it me or the town that makes you uneasy?"

Both. "I'm only trying to keep us on schedule. Media appearances are lined up for the next few days. Sergeant Major Graves also made it clear he wanted you to determine what you were cooking and to try your recipes out before the contest. He doesn't seem like a man you want to let down, so I'm going to stay on you and we'll need to stay on schedule. It's already going to be later than I'd like before we get to Denver."

"You've always been so concerned with schedules and timetables. One thing that can be said for you is that you've always been on time." He pulled in front of Ace's old Victorian house. "Even your mother said you were born right on time. She went into labor five minutes after midnight on the day the doctor said she'd have you, and a few hours later, you were born. You must have been the only infant on schedule."

"Schedules are the timetable of life. Stick to it, and you'll get everything done you were supposed to. It's all about timing."

"Madison, sometimes you need to let your hair down a little and be spontaneous. You can't plan every minute of your day." He shoved the truck into park and shut it off.

"I'm spontaneous when I want to be."

He turned enough to look at her directly, a smirk tugging up the corners of his lips. "You're spontaneous when you have it written in the calendar to be spontaneous. But for the next two weeks, you're stuck with me, and when I'm not on duty, I don't live by any schedule. You're going to have to learn to go with the flow."

"We've got interviews scheduled, a photo shoot…"

"Maddie…"

"Don't call me that." She cut him off before he could finish his sentence. Years ago, that had been his special name for her as a way to tease her about her temper, but now it only pained her to hear it. *It was my decision to leave him, so why does it hurt so much now? Hormones.*

"You'll always be my Maddie." He reached out to touch her, but stopped before he did. Instantly, he grew serious and nodded. "We'll do everything you've set up, but it doesn't mean I'll be jumping like a well-trained dog every hour for you. On the plane, I want to look at this schedule, and I don't want you to add anything else to it without consulting me."

"I'm the public relations director on this project. If I can get any more media attention for it, whether it be for you or one of the other branches, I damn well will. This is my job we're talking about."

"And my life." He tugged the keys from the ignition. "I never wanted to do this stupid cook-off. I cook for the guys because it's better than eating the crap the military tries to pass off as food. I take what we have on hand and turn it into something that's at the very least somewhat enjoyable, but I've never wanted to compete on some cooking show, or be a chef. I'm only here because I'm under direct orders from my Sergeant Major."

"It won't be so bad."

"Really?" He cocked an eyebrow at her. "Because I think it will be, or I wouldn't have offered to become a target for shooting practice."

"What?"

"When Graves told me about this new assignment my exact words were: Isn't there something my time could be better spent on? A volunteer deployment? Crash test dummy? Target for shooting practice?"

She sat there staring at him for a moment, waiting for him to tell her he was just joking, but something about the look in his eyes told her that he was dead serious. He'd rather do any of those things than this cooking competition. "I'm sorry you got dragged into this, but I had nothing to do with that. Your Sergeant Major is the one who recommended you to the brass, and they had the final choice. Don't blame me because you're saddled with me and these orders."

"I'm not upset about being stuck with you. That might be the one highlight of this situation." He opened the door and slid out. "Coming?"

Highlight. He couldn't actually mean that he wanted to spend the next two weeks with her. What about the tension that was in the air because of the way they'd left things? *Don't be stupid. The tension isn't from that. It's from the desire burning in his gaze that heats the fires within me.*

He couldn't possibly feel anything for her after more than a dozen years. Could he?

Chapter Two

Lucky leaned against the kitchen counter as he filled Ace in on his new orders, while his thoughts kept traveling back to Madison. She had refused to come in until Gwen had gone to retrieve her by force, if necessary, from the truck. Thankfully, it hadn't come to that, and now the women were chatting in the living room, while Roulette slept in her bassinet, and the men were in the kitchen. It was almost like old times except his parents weren't hiding somewhere in the house waiting to catch them in some compromising position—well, that and Roulette was here.

If things hadn't turned out the way they had so many years ago, maybe he'd have been married to Madison and living a life like Ace had with a wife and baby. Funny how things change. Only last night he was happy living the single life, enjoying his condo and freedom. Now, here he was questioning everything he thought he wanted. Though, there was one thing he knew he wanted, and that was to get her on her back. He wanted to make love to her again, to hear her scream his name in ecstasy. He missed the way she wrapped her legs around him as they made love, and how the simplest touches had her wiggling against him.

"Lucky?"

Ace's tone brought him back to reality. "Huh, what were you saying?"

"I told you I'd pick up your mail and check on your condo. Gwen and I will go over and take care of the refrigerator and stuff tomorrow. Anything else you need done?"

He tried to think, but nothing came to mind. He had a simple life. There were no plants that needed to be watered, and all of his bills were automatically deducted from his checking account, so when he was deployed he didn't have to worry about anything. "I don't think so. I'd put a stop on the mail, but we've got to catch a plane in a few hours. I barely have time to go home and pack."

"No sweat." Ace took a swig from the beer bottle. "Need a ride to the airport?"

"Naw, thanks though. I'll leave my truck there since my return flight doesn't have me getting in until late." He glanced at the clock on the stove. "I guess we should be going, I've still got to pack."

"Well, little brother, I'll be rooting for you. I know you can do it. Go there and show them what a great chef you are, all self-taught and everything."

"You better not let your team hear that. Rooting for the Marines when you're a Navy SEAL could get you stoned."

Ace grabbed his beer, and with a smirk he led the way to the living room. "You know the guys love your cooking. We'll all be rooting for you, but be prepared to pay up big time if you lose."

"I'm sure there's already a poll going on base. If I hear my very own brother bet against me, there's going to be hell to pay." A soft cry from Roulette had Lucky speeding his pace. "What's wrong, darling?" He plucked his niece from the bassinet and cradled her in his arms.

"I think she might be coming down with something. She's been fussy today and has barely slept." Gwen stifled a yawn.

"Have you been keeping your mommy up?" He kissed her forehead but it didn't feel warm.

16

"And her daddy," Ace added as he dropped like a lead balloon onto the sofa next to his wife.

"Get me out of this cooking battle, and I'll take her so you can get some sleep." He rocked her gently, easing the cries.

"You wish." Ace shook his head. "But the Marines are counting on you."

"You're going to make them proud and show them what you've got. I know you can win this if you put your mind to it," Madison announced, and as everyone turned to look at her, the heat of embarrassment colored her cheeks. "Umm, I think I'll wait outside."

"There's no need, we're going." He stepped toward the sofa, and with one final kiss, he passed Roulette off to Gwen. "Now, you behave for your mommy, but make sure you keep Daddy on his toes. Also, don't grow too much while your favorite uncle is away."

"Favorite?" Ace gave a deep chuckle. "See, she was telling me just this morning that Uncle Boom is her favorite."

"Stop it, you two; you know she has no favorites." Gwen cut them off before they could continue to provoke each other.

"Yes, ma'am." He gave his sister-in-law a mocking salute, before tipping his head toward Ace. "Keep him in line."

"These two never stop." Gwen met Madison's gaze. "Wynn will be sorry she missed you, so I hope you keep your word and come back soon. It will be nice for all of us to be back together again."

"Soon." Madison nodded and headed for the door.

"Everything okay with her?" Gwen whispered as Madison opened the front door.

"She hadn't expected that I was the Marine she'd have to work with. I believe I've thrown her for a loop. If she could board a plane in the opposite direction without putting her career on the line, I believe she would." Lucky glanced toward the door and considered his options on how to get her over this initial unease.

"Go easy on her," she warned. "It's been a long time since I saw her, and I'd like to see her again soon. Don't go messing things up so she doesn't want to risk coming back into town."

He nodded, instead of stating his doubts that she would come back here even if things went smoothly. No need to shatter his sister-in-law's hopes, not without proof. Maybe their time together would make Madison long for a reunion with her two best childhood friends. At least he could hope for their sake, and maybe a little for his own.

Madison stood near the sliding glass door to the balcony and admired the view. Lucky's condo was on the eighth floor, providing a beautiful view of the ocean, and even though it was clear that a single man lived there, she wasn't surprised with how clean the place was. Mrs. Diamond had wanted each of her children to be able to take care of themselves, including cleaning up after themselves and cooking. Maybe that was where Lucky got his talent and love for cooking.

She forced her gaze to stay focused on the ocean and the boats in the distances, instead of thinking about the life Lucky led. It was so completely different than hers. Not just because he was military and she was a government employee. But the fact that he was so carefree while she was always by the book.

If his condo had anything to say about it, he was still the same guy he had been years ago. He must still like to entertain. Otherwise, the large sectional and air hockey table would have been too much for just one person. The weights near the television reminded her once again of the dedication he had to the military. The area was relatively spotless, not that she expected anything less from Lucky. He had always been the most organized of the Diamond family, and lived on a strict timetable, making him a good fit for military life. As much as he spoke of being spontaneous, he lived as much by a timetable as she did, he just didn't admit to it as much. The times he was spontaneous were mentally scheduled in, even if he didn't realize it.

"We're cutting this closer than I'd like, since the airlines suggest we arrive two hours early for security. Why don't we grab dinner at one of the restaurants at the airport?" he asked as he tossed his garment bag over the back of the sofa.

"That's fine. Don't forget your dress uniform."

"Already packed, along with my cammies. What hotel are we staying at? Is there a pool? Because if so, I should grab my trunks."

The weight of the living arrangements hit her full force, and she turned away from the view to face him. "Actually…umm…we've got a house."

"Nice. The least the government can do is spring for a house instead of shoving us in a crummy hotel room for two weeks. Even if I'm stuck sharing a room with one of the other guys."

"It's not exactly like that." She tried again, only to have him interrupt her a second time.

"Oh, I get my own room. Even better."

She shook her head, but he didn't notice. He was too busy shoving things into his bag. Now that he'd accepted his fate, he was getting into it. "Umm, Lucky…"

"What is it?" He glanced up, his toiletry bag in hand. "You okay? You look pale. Maybe you should have a seat."

"I'm fine," she snapped. "I mean. Oh hell, what I'm trying to say is we're supposed to share the house. Each branch has a handler and their own house."

"So, Maddie, you're my handler, and though you'd rather be anywhere else in the world, you're stuck sharing a house with me. Aren't you the luckiest woman?"

"Stop calling me that."

"But you used to love it."

"That was years ago." *It didn't tear out my heart then. I was young and naïve. I found the little nickname sweet, even though it was brought on by my raging temper.* "Stuck together all day in a house. We need to at least try to get along."

"I didn't realize we weren't getting along." He tossed the toiletry bag into his larger bag. "I know you're not thrilled to be stuck with me, and I'm not happy with this competition, but we've both got a job to do, so let's do it. If you want to give me the schedule and just go your own way until we have to make public appearances, then so be it."

She'd love to take him up on that offer, or better yet skip the plane to Colorado and board one taking her back to Washington D.C. Then she could retreat to the sanctuary of her small studio apartment and try to forget about the emotions and desires he had stirred within her. But she couldn't do that. This job was her hope of making a new life and getting the bigger place she needed. It wasn't just her that she had to worry about any longer.

"Lucky, I know things are uneasy between us, but I'm not going anywhere. Since I just took this position, to see you win would do wonders for my job. So, you're stuck with me."

"I'll try not to let you down." He walked toward the kitchen and grabbed two bottles from a cabinet before returning. "Are you sure that's the only reason?"

Was she that easy to read? She wondered if he could tell that as much as she wanted to run in the opposite direction, she wanted to be near him at the same time. It was like two sides of her playing tug of war, and neither side was winning. She wasn't even sure she knew which side she wanted to win.

Ignoring his question, she nodded to the spice bottles in his hand. "What's that?"

"My secret ingredients that are going to make sure I win this competition."

"Since we go way back, do I get to know what your secret ingredients are?"

He grabbed one of the shirts from the top of the bag and carefully rolled the bottles in it before placing them inside. "One is real vanilla bean."

"What about the other?"

"Madd…" He caught himself before he called her by the nickname. "You'll have to wait to find out. Not even my family knows that one."

"As long as it wins this, you can keep your secret. Otherwise, you'll have to reveal it."

"I'd like to reveal more than just a secret."

Wouldn't we all. Thankfully, she caught herself before the words slipped out of her mouth. After all, she was keeping the biggest secret of all. Not just from him, but from everyone. Secrets had a tendency to fester in the gut until a person thought they'd explode from it.

"Are you all packed? We should be going."

"Just a minute." He went to the hall closet and pulled out a black leather jacket. "It's still cold in Denver at this time."

"Very well, let's go." She glanced at the view one final time before she grabbed her planner from the table and his garment bag with his dress uniform.

"I can get that."

"I've got nothing else to carry." She draped it over her arm. "Do you want to catch a cab?"

"We'll take my truck, and I'll leave it at the airport for when I return." He grabbed his bag and glanced at her. "I just realized something. What about your luggage?"

"This is only a long layover for me, so mine is at the airport. I didn't even pack a carry on as I normally would so I didn't have to lug it around town." She nodded to her planner. "This was all I have to worry about and it rarely leaves my sight."

"I wouldn't be surprised if you had scheduled bathroom breaks in that thing." He joked and headed toward the door.

Chapter Three

Seven hours of traveling, and the very idea the first media appearance was only a few hours away, had Lucky on edge. The same nervous energy that coursed through him before a mission was bubbling within him now. He needed something to take his mind off it.

"You okay?" Madison questioned as he grabbed their luggage from the trunk.

"Fine." He pulled her rolling suitcase from the trunk, and placed it on the ground before slinging his bag over his shoulder. "It's nearly three in the morning, so we should get settled and get some sleep."

"You don't look like you could sleep." She grabbed the garment bag and shut the trunk. "You're nervous. Just like in high school when you had to give that speech. The big bad Marine is terrified of a little press...I never thought I'd see the day."

"I don't care to be singled out for special attention. I've done nothing that would warrant this...this punishment."

She had begun to lead the way up the sidewalk to the two-story home in a small, family-friendly development, when she stopped and turned back to him. "You see this as punishment. That Sergeant Major Graves singled you out because of something you did. Whereas the rest of us see this as honoring a talent you have. There's no reason you should hide the magic you do in the kitchen."

"I only started this to bring a touch of home to us while we were away. I didn't do it to be on some competition, or for anyone else to know about it."

"Your reasoning doesn't matter. You take ordinary foods and turn them into something divine." As if realizing she wasn't changing his mind, she added, "If you can't do this for yourself, then do it for the wounded Marines this will benefit if you win. That alone should be the motivation you need."

"What's that supposed to mean?"

"A little over a year…"

"Enough." He tried to keep the regret and sadness from showing in his voice but failed miserably. "It's cold. Let's get inside."

She nodded, but didn't move. "You might want to shove that memory aside, but it's a part of you. A part of this. It's part of why Graves chose you." She slipped the door key from her pocket, and headed toward the front of the house.

"What does that have to do with this?"

She didn't answer him at first, waiting until the door opened. She flicked on the entryway light, then turned to him. "Graves didn't tell you?"

"Tell me what?" He kicked the door shut and tossed his bag on the floor. He was tired of playing twenty questions, and he was tired of the whole situation. The next two weeks would be worse than any orders he'd ever had before.

"Private First Class Kyle Phillips."

"Leave him out of this," he snapped, trying to push the memories back into the depths of his mind.

"He's the one who recommended you to Graves for this."

"What?" Anger at not knowing threatened to spill out, but it wasn't

Madison he should be angry at. It was Graves, or even Phillips. Graves never mentioned it, not that it would have made much difference. After all, an order from a commanding officer was still an order, but it mattered to Lucky.

"I'm sorry, Lucky, I thought you knew."

"Just forget it," he snapped before reining himself back. "It wouldn't have changed anything, but I'll be damn sure to have a few words with them when this is all over."

"It wasn't so much his fault. His mother and my boss are good friends. She knew of Kyle's service, and asked if he had any recommendations. That's why he went to Graves."

"I thought you didn't know who the Marine was that you were meeting? If you knew Kyle recommended the person, you had to have had a name."

She placed the garment bag over her suitcase, dug into her planner before finally finding a printout and held it out to him. "I didn't know until we were on the plane, when I read the form I received before I flew to Virginia. That's how I found out. I'd have told you, but you were trying to sleep. I didn't want to bother you." When he didn't take the paper, she placed it back on top of the planner, and set it on the entryway table. "I only know what was in the paper, but there's no wonder why he'd recommend you."

"I don't want to discuss it." He snatched his bag off the tiled floor. "I need to get some sleep."

"Take the bedroom at the end of the hall." She nodded toward the stairs. "I'll be in the one closest to the stairs if you need anything."

"I take it you've been here." He grabbed the garment bag before taking her suitcase as well. He didn't want to have to come back downstairs for anything. He needed to put some distance between them, avoid that look of sympathy in her eyes.

"I was here two weeks ago to check out rental properties. Each contestant has their own rental with a chef's dream kitchen where they'll be staying with their handlers for the next two weeks. Being that I picked them out, I assigned the nicest to myself. There's even a hot tub on the deck if you're interested. A small work space for me and a kitchen that I hope will suit your needs."

"I'm sure it's more than I'm used to. The cooking supplies were extremely limited when we were deployed." With one more glance at her, he took the first step to the second floor.

"I can take my bag," she offered, but he was already a quarter of the way up.

"Don't worry, Maddie, I won't open it and look at all your sexy lingerie. I'll be a gentleman and place it in your room."

"I'd never expect anything less from you."

After depositing her suitcase in her room, he headed farther down the hall to his room. The door was open, revealing a large, king size bed. The solid cherry wood headboard made it seem more imposing than it was, drawing attention to the warm blue accent wall behind the bed. The deep blue comforter reminded him of Ace's dress blues, only this had a sliver threading creating panels within the blanket.

He dropped his bags on the cedar chest at the foot of the bed and took in the rest of the room. There was a dresser, and what he assumed was a closet, on the same wall as the entryway. To the left was an adjoining bathroom, but it was the window that caught his attention. In the daylight, the large window would provide a stunning view of the mountains he'd noticed on the drive, but now he could only see darkness.

"If only this was a vacation instead of an assignment, I might actually be able to enjoy the mountains. Such a change from Virginia Beach," he mumbled to himself as he began to strip out of his clothes.

He crawled between the sheets in his boxers, and was no longer able to push the memories away. In a semi-conscious decision, he decided to reroute his thoughts to Madison instead of recalling Kyle, which would only lead to doubt and rage. He let his eyelids drift shut, and the memories flooded back.

Two days before he was due to report to boot camp, they'd been curled up in bed at a small bed and breakfast two towns over. He wasn't sure how he'd managed to talk her into it, but there they were.

The sun was just peeking over the horizon, and they had spent the night in each other's arms. Neither of them had slept, as if they didn't want to miss a moment of their time together. Four years dating, but friends for even longer, and yet every day had felt new and exciting. He wanted that, and he wanted her. While many of their friends had been thinking about college, and the careers they'd have, he was thinking that he wanted to spend the rest of his life with her. His plan had been to propose to her, but the moment had been so perfect he remembered not wanting to move from where he was, with her wrapped around him, to get the ring.

"Lucky…"

"Hmm." He teased his finger along the curve of her spine.

"I love you."

"Mmm." He tipped her head up toward him. "Maddie, you're the only woman for me. I love you, too." He started to kiss her when she pulled back just enough to stop him.

"Wait, there's something I need to say. Something I've wanted to say, but I wanted this time with you first. It's selfish, but I wanted to remember us like this."

"Remember us? What are you talking about? We'll be together soon."

"I'm leaving for college in two weeks, and things are going to be different. We're not going to see each other. We'll be living different lives."

He wasn't sure he liked where this was heading. "Maddie, we'll get through it. It's only for a little bit, and then you can join me once I have my duty station. You can continue with college wherever I'm stationed. I thought we discussed this."

"We did, but things have changed." She got out of bed, slipped into a long t-shirt, and went to the window. "I think we need to take a break."

"A break?" He shot up out of bed, but didn't go to her. After the night they'd shared, she wanted a break.

"I love you, Lucky, and I always will, but I think we need this. You can go to boot camp, and I can begin college."

"This is because I joined the military, isn't it?" When she remained silent, he grabbed his jeans and slipped them on. "I wouldn't have joined the Marines if I knew it meant losing you." Even as he said it, he knew it was true. She was more important to him then his desire to serve his country and follow in his family's footsteps. She was the woman he wanted by his side, and a love like that wasn't something to pass by, no matter how young they were.

"This is what you've always wanted. The Diamonds are a military family, and have been for generations. Look at Ace. He swayed from the path by becoming a Navy SEAL, but that doesn't change the fact that the military life is a part of each of you. I'd never ask you to give that up." She turned toward him. "Even so, that's not the reason. Our lives are changing and we need to make sure this is what we want."

"I already know you're what I want. I fell in love with you when we were children, and I'll never stop loving you."

"Don't you see?"

"See what?"

"We're all we've ever known. You were my first boyfriend, the first guy I kissed, and the first one I've made love to."

"I don't see the issue there." He slipped his shirt on and sat down on the bed to put his shoes on.

"I don't want there to come a day when either of us regret not having time apart." She rubbed her hands down her arms. "I'm not saying I want to be with someone else, because I don't."

"Then why are you doing this?"

"Because…" She paused as if she wasn't sure why. "I don't want this to happen once you're at boot camp. You don't need to receive a letter telling you this, so I'm doing it now."

"Your timing is impeccable." He grabbed his jacket, and as he stuck his hands into his pocket, the ring box brushed against his fingers. "After the night we had, now you want to break up."

"I'm doing this for both of us, but also to protect you. Let's just see what happens."

"Yeah, let's." He stormed from the room, thankful they had driven there separately.

"I'm sorry, Lucky."

He didn't even bother to reply, he just sped his pace. The military had been what was expected of him, and maybe he wanted it, too. But what he wanted more than his next breath was the woman in that room. She was his reason for everything.

As Lucky tossed and turned in his sleep, the vivid memory drifting in his dreams, he knew his feelings hadn't changed.

Instead of going to bed like she should have, Madison went to the kitchen for coffee and to reply to a few emails on her phone. Anything to keep herself from going upstairs only to climb into bed overcome with memories of Lucky. If it weren't at the cost of her pride, she'd trade off with one of the other handlers, just to put some distance between them. Though, if her boss got wind of it, there'd be some explaining to do.

She'd suck it up and get him through this. Two weeks…fourteen days, and then he'd be out of her life again. The *again* thought had her sinking down onto one of the living room chairs without getting her coffee, or even pulling out her phone. The morning she'd told him that she wanted a break had been the hardest morning of her life, and up until recently, it had been her only regret. Now, she had two big regrets but only one had to do with Lucky. The other was her own fault.

Over the years, she had thought about him, but after they split, it never seemed to be the right time to tell him she had made a mistake. Instead, she lived with the regret and closed herself off from Gwen and Wynn to avoid the chance she might run into him. She had tried to forget him, but he always stayed with her. Even when it came to Russell.

Russell had been the most serious relationship she'd had since Lucky, and even that had been only part-time. He was the complete opposite of Lucky, and that had been some of the draw. It had also turned out to be the flaw of their relationship as well, especially when it came to the lying aspect of it. Liars were something she couldn't move past, that and married men. Unfortunately, Russell was both.

"Forget about Russell, forget about Lucky. You need to focus on the next several months."

She let her head fall back against the chair, and her eyes closed. Instantly, memories rushed forward. She could almost picture herself in the flame red prom dress, which had a slit up to the middle of her thigh. When Lucky had picked her up, his suit and tie had matched. He had been handsome in everyday clothes, but the suit had brought out an air of danger to him.

Her mind conjured images of what he might look like in his Marine uniform, contouring to his body, showing off his well-toned muscles. Her heart beat faster at the thought. *Get control of yourself.*

Chapter Four

Morning arrived sooner than Madison would have liked. Even as she lay in bed trying to summon the strength to get up, she could hear Lucky as he moved about below. From the smell of it, he was already cooking up a storm in the kitchen. He had never been an early riser, so whatever had him up and in the kitchen at this time of the morning had to be something else. Could it be nerves?

Not able to put it off any longer, she swung her legs over the side of the bed and stood. She wanted to check on him before she showered and prepared for the day. She grabbed the heather gray cardigan from the top of her suitcase and slipped it on over her tank top and yoga pants before grabbing her cell phone from the nightstand.

On her way out of the bedroom, she glanced at her reflection in the mirror. The beginnings of dark circles were peeking through the skin under her eyes. Memories of their past together had kept her up most of the night, only to fall asleep shortly before the sun rose. Every time she closed her eyes, images of some of their dates popped into her thoughts. Even after she had gotten to sleep, memories of the two weeks between high school graduation, and that fateful morning at the bed and breakfast when she threw it all away, drifted through her thoughts.

He'd set up a romantic dinner on the rooftop of the building where he now lived. A friend of theirs, who'd graduated a few years before, had been a security guard there, and had pulled a few strings to allow them access to the rooftop deck. The dinner had been nothing compared to the views or the company. He had thought of everything, including music to dance to. Every day, he had made her feel like she meant the world to him, and that had been the hardest part of their breaking up. She loved him and never wanted it to end, but life was dividing them, sending them to separate ends of the United States. The jagged pieces of her heart were still there. Even after all these years, nothing had changed. She still loved him. Now, more than ever, she had to keep it to herself. He deserved that much from her.

Once again, she pushed her memories aside and ran her hands through her hair, pulling the long strands into a messy ponytail. "You can get through this if you just stop thinking about the past and focus on the future." Even as she said the words, she wasn't so sure. Their past was as much a part of their lives as tomorrow. It had brought them both to the place they were in now.

As she made her way downstairs, she once again wondered why she hadn't checked each of the contestants for this competition before picking one for herself. If she had investigated things further, she wouldn't have to spend the next two weeks stuck in a house with him as he prepared for the cooking showdown. Instead, she'd have only had to run into him a handful of times. Hindsight and all of that, but it didn't change anything.

As she came down the stairs, she could see Lucky at the stove. Whatever he was doing, he had his back to her and he was mumbling to himself. She couldn't make out the words, but something about his tone didn't sound happy.

"Morning," she called as she stepped off the last step.

"Morning. There's fresh coffee in the pot and breakfast will be done in a few."

"You didn't have to make me breakfast." The wood floors were cool under her feet as she made her way farther into the kitchen. Everything in her wanted to pour herself a mug of fresh coffee, but that was off limits now. Instead, she pulled open the refrigerator, grabbed the carton of orange juice, and poured herself some. It might not have the same wake-up abilities of heavenly coffee, but it was the best she could do.

"I'm supposed to be preparing, so here I am." He placed a crepe onto the plate, tossed on a few raspberries, and grabbed another pan from the stove. "Crepe with fresh cream and raspberries. Along with a crab, red pepper, and onion omelet with a drizzle of rich hollandaise sauce."

"Sounds delicious." Even if it was more then she normally had in the mornings. Toast and coffee had been her morning routine for years.

"Sit, eat."

"You're not joining me?" She accepted the plates he held out to her.

"Not now, I've got to finish the mousse."

"Mousse?"

"Black Tie Mousse Cake. It's one of my specialties, and I figured if there's a dessert part then I needed to brush up on my recipe since I haven't made it in a few months."

She took a seat at the bar so she could watch him. "There are three rounds. Appetizers, main course, and dessert. For appetizers, each competitor will be required to complete two separate ones. One of them will be with a mystery ingredient."

"Mystery ingredient." He turned to look at her. "Crap, I hadn't considered that. Will that be an issue each round?"

"No. We've decided that since none of you are professional chefs who do this for a living, we wouldn't make it that difficult for you. Only the appetizer round will have that, and only one of them will require it."

"Then why do it at all?"

"It's to throw each of you off-balance, to see how well you do under pressure. Well, pressure in the kitchen." She took a bite of the omelet and almost moaned in pleasure. His cooking skills had been good before, but it seemed that over the years they had grown to a whole new level. If this omelet with the hollandaise sauce was anything like he'd prepare for the judges, he was sure to win.

"Good?"

"Better than good." She took another bite and let her eyes close. "Mmm…this sauce is delicious."

"That's an old Diamond recipe with a few *Lucky* changes." He smirked. "Besides the appetizer round, are there any other conditions?"

"Not really. Only that you have to prepare the food before the judges. We'll shop for whatever supplies you need for your three choices that morning. One hour before we begin, you'll find out your mystery ingredient and we'll have someone standing by for a grocery run if need be."

"Where will I be cooking? Will I be able to go over the kitchen and supplies before the actual day of the event?"

"You've already seen the kitchen." With a fork full of crepe, she tipped her head toward the kitchen behind him.

"What? They're not doing this in one location? How is it to be judged fairly, then? Wouldn't that mean there'd be different judges?"

The questions flew at her before she had time to answer them. When he finally stopped, she took one last bite, and set her fork on the edge of the plate. "Unless we spent a couple thousand dollars, we weren't able to rent one of the television studios with kitchens like on all those cooking shows. So, we decided to save the money. Because of that, we were able to offer a higher prize for the wounded veterans. Each house is well equipped, and we'll be doing everything here. If there's anything that's missing, we'll get it."

"What about judging?"

"Everyone will have their own timeframes, and the judges will go from house to house. This won't be televised. Well, not the whole thing. I've pulled a few strings and was able to get a news reporter here. She'll do a collective piece with snippets from each house. There will be additional news reports for the one who wins."

"If this was supposed to shine the military in a different light, why not televise it?"

She polished off the last bite of the omelet before answering. "Cost and time, mostly. It would require at least an hour spot, and would have been an expensive, time consuming undertaking to have national television exposure. My boss decided that since this was the first test in the new campaign, she wanted to play it safe. There's a still photographer who will be recording every second so we can use it for marketing."

He grabbed a bag of sugar from the cabinet and opened it. "What about the media appearances you mentioned?"

"Each contestant will be interviewed and photographed beforehand. Some will appear on news coverage while others will wait, and only the winner's interviews will be broadcast." Even though she was full, she stabbed another raspberry and remembered the second part of this whole thing.

"What's wrong?"

"Umm…" She had been so preoccupied with seeing him again that she had forgotten what happened if he won. *I can't hope he loses just so I don't have to spend more time with him. That's selfish, and he deserves better than that from me.*

"Earth to Madison. What did you just think of?"

"Part two of this whole campaign." She pushed the rest of the crepe away. "The winner and handler are off on another two weeks of media engagements with both televised and print interviews."

"Four weeks…" He set the bowl aside that he was hand mixing something in. "Four weeks stuck in this nightmare."

"Oh, come on, Lucky, it's not that bad."

"It might not be for you, but this isn't the reason I joined the Marines. It's sure as hell not the reason I started cooking. I want to be back on base, training with my men, hell…even going on a deployment." He leaned against the counter and looked at her. "When I offered to be used for target practice, or as a crash test dummy, I didn't realize how much I'd prefer those options over this. Now, I do."

"What does that mean? Are you pulling out?" She tried not to think about how that would look on her record. That she couldn't even keep her very first assignment on track, or even her own competitor from throwing in the towel before it even began. If she lost this job, she wasn't sure what she was going to do.

"No." He let out a deep sigh. "Even if I wanted to, I couldn't. Graves knew I wouldn't do this of my own free will, so he decided to make it a direct order. I might not be court marshaled for it since, after all, it's supposed to be volunteers who are doing this, but there would be some serious hell to pay. Those consequences are not something I'm eager to endure. So, I'll see this through."

"It won't be so bad. In a few weeks you can be back on base, doing what you normally do."

"Damn right." He grabbed the bowl and began to whisk the contents again. "Because in two weeks, I'll be back in Virginia. There's not a chance I'm going to win this."

"You'd sabotage yourself?" If her boss found out, she'd be the one in hot water and possibly out of work.

"I don't think I'm the best one to win this. I'm not a damn chef, I'm a Marine."

She hadn't missed that he had avoided answering her question directly. Even if he was upset he'd been chosen, she couldn't see him screwing it up just to get out of it. "If you weren't a Marine, you'd make one fine chef." She nodded to the plates before her. "You should remember I'm not a breakfast person, let alone someone who enjoys eggs, but I finished that omelet. It was delicious. You were always a good cook, you get that from your mother, but over the years it seems you've improved."

"When you're a bachelor, you have to cook or you'll starve. There are only so many times a person can eat out before they get tired of the food choices."

There was a silence that fell over them as she gathered her dishes and began to clean up. After she had them in the dishwasher, she sat back down at the bar. "Lucky…this might not mean much to you, but before you sabotage yourself, think about Kyle and the other Marines who could use the money you'd win."

"Guilt is a powerful thing when used properly. Mom always went to guilt when nothing else worked. Even Graves used it to get me here." He pulled out another bowl and began adding ingredients to it. "As much as I hate being a part of this, I'm not one to admit defeat. I'll give this my best because my fellow brothers and sisters in arms deserve that from me. If I sabotaged it, I would be hurting them, not myself, and that's not my style. Don't worry, I'll play along and keep your precious game flowing on schedule."

"This isn't about me." She took a sip of her orange juice and tried to settle her nerves. "This is an awkward situation, I get it, but you can do a good thing here. Exposure for the military is never a bad thing and the money for those wounded Marines…"

"Just stop. I said I would do it."

Before she could respond, her cell phone rang. She pulled it out of the pocket of her cardigan, and glanced at the screen. "Excuse me, I have to take this." She hopped off the bar stool, headed for the small office space on the other side of the living area, and brought the phone to her ear. "Hi, Mom."

"Don't *hi Mom* me. You couldn't even send me a text to let me know you arrived in Denver safely? Your plane could have crashed, and I'd never know."

"Mom…" She shook her head and smiled. "It was after three in the morning here when I arrived. I was exhausted, and I'm not a teenager anymore. You don't have to worry about me."

"You'll find out soon enough that you'll never stop worrying about your child, no matter how old they are."

She refused to think about her mom's statement. She cleared her throat. "So, Mom, did you just call to see if I arrived? After all, I'm sure you already have the news on and know that a plane didn't crash. So, you knew I was safe."

"Not that you bothered calling," her mother reminded her before diving into the real reason she'd called. "Did you pick up your Marine?"

"Yeah, and Mom…" She closed the door and moved to the far side of the room, next to the window.

"What is it, hon?"

"It's Lucky." The first tear she had allowed herself rolled down her cheek. "Lucky Diamond."

Chapter Five

Lucky spent most of the day cooking, testing out different recipes. He wasn't sure what they were going to do with all the food, but if he was going to have a fighting chance, he needed to be prepared. Keeping busy had kept his thoughts away from the person that had brought him here, but as the day dwindled, he was having a harder time keeping the memories at bay. Images of Kyle popped into his thoughts, and each time they were harder to shove back into the mental box where he kept them.

The front door opened and a second later closed, announcing Madison's return. She had been gone most of the afternoon checking on the other contestants, leaving him time to work without interruption. It also gave him time to consider where things stood with them. He wanted her as much now, if not more, than he had years ago, but he had no idea how to start. There wasn't a wedding ring on her finger, which surprised him. He would have thought she'd have settled down years ago, with a husband and a few children. Even without a ring, there could be someone waiting for her back in Washington D.C.

"Lucky?"

"I'm here." He placed a stuffed chicken breast on a plate.

"You're still cooking?" She placed her laptop bag and planner on the counter. "I figured you'd have called it a night by now."

"Since tomorrow is full of media appearances, I wanted to make sure I got through some different recipes today." He placed the second chicken breast on the other plate. "I guess you could say dinner's done. Stuffed chicken breast just came off the stove, so we'll eat that, but there's some other things I want you to try and give me your thoughts on. I need some feedback before I decide what to make."

"It looks delicious."

"Thanks." He grabbed some grilled asparagus and added it to the plate before drizzling some of the hollandaise sauce that was left over from breakfast over it. "There are seven different appetizers to test as well. I'd have started with those, but this is hot and ready."

"It's fine. I'll grab drinks. What would you like?"

"I saw beer in there earlier; I'll take one of those." He took the plates to the table, instead of the bar where she had breakfast that morning. "Is everything okay?"

She poured herself a glass of water and added a slice of lemon to it before grabbing his beer. "Yes. Everyone arrived and has settled in, so everything is going according to plan. I've got to meet with my boss tomorrow between two of your interviews, so if you wouldn't mind accompanying me, it would be easier than coming back here to drop you off and then pick you up again."

"Whatever you need." He untwisted the beer cap and waited for her to sit down. "Though that's not what I meant. I wasn't asking if the others had arrived with their handlers."

"Then what did you mean?" She cut into the chicken breast and took a bite. "This is enchanting. What's in it? Are those almonds?"

"It's stuffed with artichoke hearts, spinach, almonds, and parmesan cheese."

"You make this for a bunch of Marines?" She took another bite. "I just picture this more at a dinner party or in a fancy restaurant."

"Just because we're supposed to be a bunch of big bad Marines doesn't mean we don't enjoy the finer foods." He speared a bite of the chicken but didn't bring it to his mouth. "I believe you're avoiding the subject. I know even with your deflection that you knew what I meant when I asked if things were okay. You've been off-kilter since you got off the phone with your mother. Are your parents okay?"

"Oh yeah, they're fine. They moved to Florida…but I guess you already knew that."

"I know." He didn't bother to mention that the reason he knew was because their house went on the market and he had bought it. All those years ago, he'd snatched it up because he thought she'd come back to him. When she did, the house she had loved and the place they had so many good memories in would be theirs. When he realized she wasn't coming back, he couldn't bring himself to move in, or even sell it. Instead, he had rented it out to a family that had lived on base but wanted to have a place of their own without buying. Three and half years they had been there, but in a few months they were changing duty stations and the place would be vacant. This time, he promised himself he'd put it on the market and close the door to the past. That was before Maddie came strolling back into his life.

They ate a few bites in silence while he hoped she'd just tell him what was bothering her, so he wouldn't have to pull it out of her. In the end, his patience ran out. He set his fork down, and leaned back from the table. "Since that phone call, you've been uneasy. Almost like you can't stand to be in the same room as me. So, what is it? Did your mother say something about me that upset you?"

"Mom has nothing to do with this." She cut the asparagus into bite size pieces and then cut it down further. Distracting herself with her food to avoid the subject at hand.

"Then what is it? Last night, things were fine…even this morning over breakfast. Now there's a tension in the air. It won't be pleasant to spend the next thirteen days like this, but if you wish—"

She dropped her fork on the plate, and the clash of it against the dish cut him off. "How am I supposed to pretend we don't have history? Every time I look at you, I wonder what would have happened if I'd done things differently."

"Are you implying you regret your decision?" He almost couldn't believe her words. He had regrets from that day, and the days following. If he had a chance to go back and do it all over again, he'd fight for her with everything he had. His only excuse for not fighting for her was that he'd been young and stupid. He had allowed his anger to get the best of him. He'd thought by stepping away and giving her time, she'd come back to him. When she didn't, too much time had passed for him to just show up at her doorstep and expect to get her back.

"Yes…no…oh hell."

"Well, which is it?" He watched her, waiting for her final answer.

"What does it matter? It's not something that can be changed. Regret or no regret, it still doesn't allow us to go back and change things."

"It matters to me." He leaned forward and placed his hand over hers. The simple touch was something he had longed to do since they were in Graves's office. "What if you could go back and change things, would you? Would you still do what you did?"

"I've thought about it before. Yes, I would have changed things given a second chance…but that time has passed."

"Maybe it hasn't." He couldn't keep the hope from his tone, so instead of going further, he changed his tactic. "Tell me why. Why did you end things?"

"Lucky, this isn't going to help either of us."

"I deserve to know. Was it because I joined the Marines? If so, why didn't you do it when I signed the papers? You knew it had always been my plan, but maybe something changed. Why the hell wait until the bed and breakfast after our night together?"

Her eyes glossed over with tears, and he wanted to take back his words. He wanted to tell her that he didn't need to know, but that would have been a lie. It was the one question he had wanted answered for years. He wanted to know why she had done it. What had suddenly changed that made their relationship no longer worth fighting for?

She pushed back from the chair, went to the window, and stared out. Something about the way she looked didn't make it seem as though she was admiring the mountains, but instead picturing the day in question. "You were off to Parris Island, South Carolina, and I was about to start college in Boston. We were going to be more than just a few hours' drive away from each other. A plane trip. Even then, it wasn't like either of us could have just visited the other when we were lonely. After boot camp, we had no idea where you'd be stationed. You could have come back to Virginia, or you could have been sent to San Diego. Either way, we were going to be apart for some time."

"I know, but what I don't understand is what the change was. We discussed that. You should have known I would have come to Boston anytime I got leave, and you could have come to see me wherever I was stationed. We'd have made it work."

"I wanted to remember us how we were, the love we had for each other. I didn't want to end things on a bad note."

He nearly spit out the beer he had just drank. "What?"

"Things were so perfect between us. All our friends thought we were the perfect couple. Our parents thought we'd get married." She turned back toward him. "With all the distance that would have separated us, we could have drifted apart. If things were going to end, I wanted them to end with only happy memories. Nothing negative or less than we deserved. I did it because I loved you, and though it might not make sense now that we're older and wiser, I did it to protect what we had."

"That was…" He wanted to say senseless, but it would have been rude.

"I know." She nodded as if she realized what he wanted to say. "It doesn't make sense now, but when I did it I thought I was saving us both heartache."

"Instead, it only brought us broken hearts and pain. All those years we've wasted." He raised an eyebrow at her. "What are you going to do about it now?"

"What do you mean? There's nothing I can do about the past."

"I don't mean about the past, and you know that. Why don't we stop beating around the bush? I still care for you…I'd say I still love you, but I have a feeling that would scare you." He nodded to her left hand. "You're not married, and from the way you're looking at me, I'd say you don't have someone waiting for you when this is all over. So, what's stopping us from exploring this? We could see what we lost when you took the decision into your own hands."

"There's nothing we can do. Our time has passed." She turned on her heels, and left the room.

"Bullshit. We were brought together for a reason. Call it fate or call it what you'd like, but this time I'm not giving up on you," he called after her as she left, determined to fight for the chance they should have had years ago.

Stripped out of her business clothes and into something more comfortable, Madison sat on the only chair in the room with her legs folded under her and her hand resting on her stomach. Over and over she kept telling herself their time had passed, that there was nothing they could go back to. She wished things were different, but they weren't. This was her life, but she'd be damned if she'd force someone else to become tangled into how things were.

"Maddie…" Lucky stood in the doorway. "Can we talk?"

"There's nothing to say. The path that would have led us together is closed."

"Why are you so adamant that things are over between us?" When she didn't answer, he strolled forward and pushed again. "Tell me the truth and I'll let things go."

"I'm pregnant."

"What?" He leaned against the dresser and watched her. "So, there is someone else. Why didn't you tell me?"

"There's no one." She pulled her legs out from under her and stretched them out. "The father doesn't even want anything to do with my child. He's…he's married."

"Oh, Maddie."

"Don't feel sorry for me," she snapped. "I did what I did. Though I might have been naïve to believe he'd leave his wife in the end, I made my choices and no one else but me has to live with that decision."

"Leave his wife?" Lucky shook his head. "I thought you'd be smarter than to get involved with a married man."

"If you must know, I didn't know he was married when things started. We were together for over a year before I found out he was married. That was two weeks before I found out I was pregnant. I told him I wouldn't be the other woman that I deserved better than that, but he strung me along for a bit longer, promising to leave his wife so we could be together. I loved him, and for those two weeks I hung on, hoping he was telling me the truth. In the back of my mind, I knew that if he left her, one day I would be the one he was cheating on. I'd have never been able to trust him. When I found out I was pregnant, that's when things ended."

"Why?"

"He said he'd never leave his wife for me, and that he wanted me to have an abortion. I refused. This baby shouldn't have to suffer because of my mistakes. I had a lawyer draw up papers for him to sign, giving up any rights he would have to the child, and in turn I would never name him as father or seek out child support."

"It's his child. He should be held responsible."

She shook her head. "I learned too late, but he's not the father I'd want for my son or daughter."

He went to her and knelt in front of her. "Shit, Maddie, you deserve so much better than this. I could beat the shit out of that bastard for leading you on when he was married, and for even suggesting that."

"Things happen for a reason, but I'll make a life for my child." She didn't pull away when he laid his hand over hers. "Don't look so worried about me. I'll be fine."

"I've no doubt that you will be, but it doesn't change my concern for you. Maddie, why does that mean we should miss this chance?"

"Did you miss that I'm pregnant? I can't ask you or anyone else to go down that road with me. This is my responsibility and I'll deal with it."

He squeezed her hand. "Pregnant or not, it doesn't change anything."

"Lucky, please…"

"Please what?" He rubbed his thumb along her knuckles.

"Don't do this." The first tear rolled down her cheek. "I've accepted what's happened between us, and what I've made of my life. Don't give me false hope for something that can never happen between us."

"Why can't it happen? Because you're pregnant?"

"Yes." That one simple word shattered her heart into even smaller pieces.

"That doesn't change things for me. We missed a chance years ago, but now we've been given a new opportunity. I've always believe you have to live life to the fullest, and that means never missing an opportunity."

"In less than six months, I'm going to be a single mother. There's no time for dating." The image of him with Roulette popped into her thoughts, and there was a brief moment in which she wished that it were her son or daughter he would be holding. The care and love he exuded when cradling his niece in his arms almost made her wish she had the courage to explore where things might go between them.

"I'm going to tell you something that isn't common knowledge." He reached to his back pocket, pulled out his wallet, and flipped it open until a picture of Ace, Gwen, and Roulette was before her. "Remember the comment you made about Roulette having the Diamond family eyes?"

"Sure. She has the same blue eyes with those dark eyelashes as the rest of the family. Anyone who knows the family would notice that."

"That might be so, but what people don't know is that Roulette is *not* Ace's biological daughter."

"What?" She looked down at the picture, and she couldn't believe it. Roulette looked more like Ace than she looked like Gwen. "That's not possible."

"It is." He leaned one knee on the floor, but didn't get up from where he knelt. "I guess it's been almost three years now, since Gwen was in that nasty car accident, and was in a coma for weeks."

"I remember that. She was living in Nashville, Tennessee working for the law office of Madison and Stine as a virtual legal researcher, when that happened. I made a point to visit her while she was in the coma, and a few times after she woke up. But how does that relate? Is that when Ace came back into her life?" She hated that she knew so little about her best friend's life. Despite years apart, she still considered Gwen and Wynn her best friends. Since then, there had never been anyone else she felt she could confide in. Even though she knew they had both married, she knew very little about their lives now. It was almost as devastating as having to deny herself Lucky's touch again.

"When she woke, she realized there was so much more in life. More that she wanted. She wasn't in a relationship, didn't even want to be because she was still in love with Ace, but she wanted a child. So, she went to a fertility clinic. That was four months before she came back to Virginia Beach, and Ace came home early from a mission to find she was living in his house."

"Roulette's father is a sperm donor? Gwen was artificially inseminated? No way."

"You can ask her yourself." He flipped his wallet closed. "She always wanted children, and she didn't want to wait any longer. At that point, she believed she'd never find love again, so she was taking life into her own hands."

"Why are you telling me this?"

"I'm telling you because you've seen firsthand the love Ace has for Roulette. Even with Gwen's pregnancy, it didn't stop what was between them. So, why are you using this as an excuse for not giving us a second chance?"

She ran her hand over her stomach. "I didn't decide to do this on my own. I made the choice to be with someone…"

"Someone who lied to you and couldn't be the man you needed. That doesn't mean all men will be the same. You didn't think we could make it work before, and maybe I'm partially to blame for that as well because I didn't fight hard enough to prove we could do it. I'm not letting you make that same decision for both of us again. Not without a fight."

"This isn't the same situation as Ace and Gwen."

"Who the hell cares about the situation?" He shook his head. "I told you about them because you seem to think that I wouldn't love this baby because I'm not the biological father. There are many stepparents in this world who are better parents than those who brought them into this world. Don't use that as an excuse not to give us both something we want."

"I'm not going to saddle you with a child because of a decision I made." She ran her hand over her stomach. Even though it was nothing more than the beginnings of a pregnancy bump, it made her feel closer to her baby. "What happened between Russell and I was a mistake, but the baby that came from that union wasn't. I will provide my child with a good life."

"I'm not doubting that, but there's no reason you should have to do it alone." He took hold of her hand and stood, taking her with him. His wallet fell to the floor, but neither of them cared. "I've thought about this since you walked into Graves's office. I want you in my life. If I have to leave the Marines, I'll do it if it means getting you back. All I'm asking for is a second chance."

She couldn't believe it, but this time it was harder to walk away from him than it had been before. She wasn't sure she could even get the words out, because all she wanted to do was fall into his embrace. To spend a few hours just being held by him, the way he used to do when they were spending an evening together. "Lucky, I don't…"

He stopped her before she could finish her sentence. "You said in less than six month you'll be a mother. Well, that will give us a chance before the baby is even born. A chance for me to fight for you, and for you to decide if you want me in your life. If you decide you don't want this relationship, the baby will never even know. Give us a chance, and if you decide you want nothing more to do with me, I'll step back and let you live your life however you want."

"I don't know."

"Just think about it." He leaned forward and kissed her cheek. "I've never stopped loving you, Maddie. We deserve a second chance."

She watched as he stepped away from her, picked up his wallet, and without another word he strolled out of her bedroom. Just like the last time he'd walked away from her, at that bed and breakfast, she wanted to stop him. She wanted to call out to him and tell him she never stopped loving him, either, but she didn't. She needed to think about it before she let herself go down that path again. It wasn't just her she had to worry about. She had to consider her child as well.

# Chapter Six

The next day had come in a rush, one interview after another, but now that it was all over, Lucky just wanted to get Madison alone. He wanted to know if she'd thought about what he had said, and if she'd come to any decision. He suspected that she had something on her mind because throughout the day she had tried to talk to him, but they got interrupted each time. Now that they were back at the house, he planned to corner her and any ringing phones be damned. He wanted to know where things stood.

"Maddie, we need to talk."

She slipped off her heels and let out a sigh that could only be associated with relief. "I was thinking the same thing, but first I want…" She paused and her lips curled into a half smirk. "Normally, I'd have filled that in with a glass of wine, but I'm playing everything by the book with this pregnancy. No caffeine, no alcohol, nothing bad for the baby will pass my lips."

"How about I make it up to you with a chocolate milkshake, extra thick, just like you like it?"

"That's better than wine, any day. I never could turn down chocolate milkshakes and…well, I crave anything chocolate."

"If you want to change, I'll make them and then we can talk."

"My clothes are fine for a bit longer, it was the heels that were killing me." She followed him into the kitchen and hopped up onto the counter, her legs swinging as she grabbed an apple from the basket. "I know you don't like the spotlight, but you did great today."

"Thanks." He grabbed the ice cream, milk, and chocolate syrup from the refrigerator. "I just want to get through this and be out of the spotlight."

"I still believe you'll win, so you'll have two additional weeks of this…if not longer."

He slid the blender from its hideaway. "You didn't always look on the dark side of things," he joked.

"Oh, come on, would it really be that bad?" She bit into the apple, and raised an eyebrow. "Would it be that bad to be stuck with me?"

"Does that mean you've given *us* some thought?" Before she could answer, the doorbell rang, interrupting them again. "Damn it. I thought when we got back here we'd finally be able to talk."

"The other contestants wouldn't come here, so it's either my boss or one of the neighbors. Either way, it shouldn't be long." She hopped off the counter. "I'll get it, you make my shake."

"You might have been given a reprieve, but I still want an answer once you get rid of them."

She didn't reply, but gave him one of her bright smiles and headed to the door. While she was gone, he busied himself making the milkshakes. If there was another interruption, be it the phone or door, he was going to pin her against the wall with his body just to get her to answer his question.

With the milkshakes in the glasses, he grabbed a piece of rich chocolate and grated some on top. Everything was perfect until he turned and found her standing there looking pale. "Maddie, what is it? Are you okay? Who was at the door?" He went to her, placing his hands on her arms because he wasn't sure if she was going to pass out. The blood appeared to have drained from her face.

"I didn't know. I swear, I didn't have anything to do with it." She stared up at him, sympathy in her eyes.

"With what?" He was still completely confused.

"I didn't know they'd bring him here. I'm sorry. Oh Lucky, I'm so sorry."

"Who?"

"Kyle."

He knew he was probably pale, too, because he could feel the color draining from his face. The memories he had tried to push away slammed into him at once, no longer willing to be denied. They crashed into him like waves onto the shore, each one growing stronger and stronger.

They had been following a lead that should have led them straight to one of the terrorists they had been searching for. With each mile, his unease worsened. It was a set up. From the passenger seat of the lead vehicle, he scanned the surroundings. The order to abort on the tip of his tongue when gunfire broke out in nearly every direction, leaving no place to take cover. Private First Class Weber was returning fire from the turret but the insurgent numbers were too great. Surrounded, he had to get them out of there or they were all dead.

"Gunny?" Corporal Juan Torres, the Humvee driver, nodded toward the roadblock before them.

"Fuck." He wasn't sure Torres had even heard it over the gunfire. "Reverse. Fall back. Now!"

Torres slammed the Humvee into reverse and plowed backward. On the radio Lucky ordered the two additional Humvees to fall back. Blood dripped down from the turret. Weber was hit but there was nothing he could do for him.

Doc, their corpsman was in the second Humvee. If they could get out of the ambush, he'd be able to help Weber. Meanwhile it was Lucky's job to keep the insurgents from gaining on his team. He had to find a way out of the ambush. Even injured Weber was firing, making each shot count, but there was too much blood. Weber wasn't going to last long up there.

"Swing left and turn us around." Lucky ordered as they neared a clearing without anyone blocking the way. They were nearly there. Just a little further and they'd be out of

range. Above him the machine gun fire stopped and Phillips helped the now unconscious Weber back into the Humvee.

With a hard left Torres had them facing the right way and Lucky could see the two other Humvees had done the same. They were dealing with less incoming gunfire and were holding their own. It was one less thing to worry about as Phillips took Weber's place in the turret and began returning fire on the insurgents who were still a threat. One moment the noise was deafening and then the next the assault subsided, only Phillips's machine gun continued.

Torres was nearing the road again after their off road adventure to get turned around. Lucky scanned the perimeter, every insurgent that had been there had moved back. Something wasn't right.

He had barely had time to register the change in their surroundings when an IED exploded, sending their Humvee skyward. He didn't have time to yell to Phillips to get inside. As they were tossed through the air, he cursed himself for going off the main road to speed their retreat to find cover.

Each second seemed like minutes as they were tossed around in the Humvee before it finally landed on its side. Lucky was pressed against the door, hurt but it could have been worse. Torres remained in his seat, thanks to the seatbelt, and blood dripped from a gash on his head. Unconscious Weber had been tossed around but he wasn't the only one. Phillips...

"Where the hell is Phillips?"

"Gunny..." Torres stared just ahead of the Humvee to where the PFC laid.

"Fuck." Lucky grabbed his rifle from the rack near the door hinge. "Get out. We've got to take cover before they open fire again."

The rest of the convoy was just ahead. Doc was in there and he'd see to Phillips. Once they were out, they could determine Weber's condition. Torres grabbed hold of the door and unhooked his belt. Within seconds they were out. "Get Weber, I'll see to Phillips." He didn't wait for the Corporal to respond before heading to the PFC. Blood coated the sand around him. He lost too much blood but that what was more shocking was what was missing.

"Lucky." She touched his arm.

Without thinking, he reached out and clasped her wrist roughly, instantly spotting the panic in her eyes. He loosened his grip but the damage had already been done. When he pulled his hand back from her, the red imprint he had left behind screamed at him. "Fuck."

"I'm sorry. I didn't know my boss had brought him here. The interview for tomorrow…they want both of you. She didn't mention it."

"That's not what I meant." He tipped his head toward her wrist. "Look what I did to you."

"It's nothing." She pulled down the sleeve to her sweater, covering the mark.

"The hell it isn't. I'm trying to convince you to give us a shot and I do something like that." He focused on the mark on her wrist because it meant he could push back the memories of Kyle and that day, but even that wouldn't stop the fact he would have to face the man who'd lost both his left leg and arm, the man who'd been burned along most of his left side, including his face. The man who'd been crippled because of him.

"Stop, Lucky." She reached out to him but stopped mid-motion.

"See, now you're too scared to touch me. The damage by that move will shatter whatever chance I had with you."

"That's not why I stopped." She took a deep breath and let it out again. "If I touch you now, I might not be able to stop myself. This…" She held up her wrist as if he needed a reminder. "Means nothing. I could see you weren't here, just lost in your memories, and I knew better than to touch you, but I did because I couldn't stop myself. The pain in your eyes as you remembered what happened to him was unbearable. I don't know the whole story, and I doubt that I ever will, but after I told you Kyle was the one who recommended you, I did some research. I found out what little I could, but because of the way you looked when I mentioned he was here, I know there's more. Maybe one day you'll tell me, and maybe you won't, but that doesn't change us."

"How can it not?"

55

"Because I know you'll never hurt me or this baby. I love you, Lucky." Tears glistened in her eyes. "Now, he's waiting outside."

"You left him outside?"

"It was his idea. He could tell by the fact I didn't know who he was that we hadn't been told he'd arrived a few hours ago, or that he was even coming. He wanted me to have a few minutes to prepare you."

Even with notice, he wouldn't have been prepared. It had been more than a year since he'd seen or even heard from Kyle. That last visit at the hospital, Kyle had told him not to return, that he could no longer look at his Gunnery Sergeant. He felt he'd failed him. To Lucky, Kyle had never failed, but the young Private First Class wouldn't listen. He wanted to wallow in the guilt and grief, and nothing Lucky could say would change that. The PFC had lost a friend and sustained injuries that would change his life forever, but it was Lucky who had to deal with the guilt of making the decision to go off road to retreat. His decision had changed the lives of many that day.

"Let's go let him in."

She shook her head and stepped aside. "You go. I think the two of you need a bit of time to yourselves. I'm going to take my milkshake into the office. When you're done, find me."

He stood there for a moment and watched as she grabbed the milkshake before strolling toward her office. Everything in him wanted to stop her, pull her into his arms, and kiss her, but he needed to face Kyle. He promised himself Maddie would be his reward. *I'm coming for you, Maddie, and you're going to be mine.*

He pulled open the front door, and there before him was the Marine he'd once thought was gone for good. A smile stretched across his face, and he was standing. The changes a year made. He almost didn't believe it was Kyle, but the sea green eyes were unmistakable.

"Shocked that I'm here?" When Lucky didn't say anything, Kyle proceeded. "The last time I saw you, I was ready to give up. I didn't see any reason for living. Not when I was down to one arm and one leg. I was half the man I was, but that all changed."

"I can't believe it." Lucky stepped back. "Come in."

"Well, believe it. I'm alive because of you. Your parting words had me so angry that they called in someone to speak with me."

Lucky shut the door before turning back to him. "I'm not sure why I'm to credit for you being alive."

"Because four months ago I married her. She came into my life to ease the anger, guilt, and regret. She showed me I was still a man, and she fell in love with me. If it wasn't for you turning my self-pity into anger, I'd have never met her, and wouldn't be here."

"Here…as in Colorado, and doing this competition?" He let out a deep laugh and shook his head. "Damn, I should have kept my mouth shut and let you kill yourself."

"Gunny, there are plenty of Marines who could use the ten thousand you could win for them, and there's no one better to do this than you." Kyle waited until they were in the living room, and had taken seats, before adding, "I nominated you for this not as some payback, but because we need someone like you fighting for us."

"I cooked for you guys because I enjoyed it. I never wanted any recognition for it."

He nodded, and leaned back on the sofa. "I've learned sometimes we don't get what we want, but in the end it turns out better than you expected."

I guess I can't blame him too much. After all, it brought me Maddie.

They spent the next hour talking, all the while avoiding the subject of their last mission together. They talked about the competition, Kyle's new wife, and even the Colorado Mountains. Finally, Kyle leaned forward and said, "You know I don't blame you, right?"

Oh, hell! Lucky wanted to contradict the statement, but after the last hour, he couldn't. It didn't matter to him if Kyle blamed him, because Lucky blamed himself. His men were his responsibility, and that day had not only left Kyle with missing body parts and burns, but it had also killed one of his Marines. Another Private First Class, on his first deployment, was killed and had left behind a wife and son. That man's blood was on his hands, and he'd have to live with the fact he hadn't ordered Torres to turn the Humvee around and wait for reinforcements the minute his intuition had kicked in.

Chapter Seven

Madison sat in front of her laptop, not really working, just waiting. Nothing happened. She had expected Lucky to come find her after he had shown Kyle out, but that had been over twenty minutes ago. He still hadn't come to the office. She was growing more impatient with each passing minute. The desire to find out what had happened between them, and to make sure he was okay, was nearly overwhelming.

Not willing to wait any longer, she rose from behind the desk and headed for the door. The house seemed eerily quiet. She looked around the first floor, but no one was there. His milkshake had been discarded on the counter, never touched. The hairs on the back of her neck stood up, warning her that something was wrong. Where was he? It was so unlike him to say he was doing something, and then not actually do it. Had the visit with Kyle upset him?

She didn't see him on the first floor, and doubted he'd be outside since his jacket was still flung over one of the bar stools in the kitchen. She headed upstairs in search of him. If he was upset about seeing Kyle, she needed to know, because tomorrow he'd have to face him again, but in an interview. One that was sure to awaken the memories even more than they had already been. She needed to find out if they would need to work something else out, or if he could keep it together long enough to get through it, and this competition.

"Lucky." She called out to him as she reached the top of the stairs. Even after receiving no response, she continued toward the master bedroom at the end of the hall.

The door was open, so she peeked in and saw him in the middle of the bed fully dressed with his eyes shut. She crept closer, and as she neared the bed, she noticed how rigid his body was. He wasn't just lying there to take a nap, he was thousands of miles away, back in Iraq fighting for this country.

She came to the side of the bed but didn't reach out to him. She had learned her lesson last time, and even though she didn't blame him for the mark on her wrist, she'd be more careful in the future. "Lucky?"

"Maddie, just go away."

"No." Now that he knew she was there, and who she was, she sat down on the edge of the bed, his hip only a few inches away. "I need to know if you're okay. If you can do tomorrow, or if I should see about making other arrangements."

"You said you were in charge of this. That your boss had given you the responsibility to make sure this went off without any problems. How could you not know she sent Kyle here?"

The pain in his voice made her feel worse than she already did. "After I left the office, she looked over the files of each contestant. That's when she read who put your name into this. The brass got the final choice, but it was Kyle and Graves who threw your name to them. She wanted to know why they pressed so hard for you to be the one they chose."

"I thought there was very little in the file about what happened."

"That's true, but she called Sergeant Major Graves, and that's when she learned the story. She wanted to—"

"Exploit it?" he supplied when she stumbled over what word to use.

She nodded, even though he couldn't see it because his eyes were still closed. "I'm sorry. I didn't know anything about it until he showed up at the door."

"For the two minutes you were at the door, you sure learned a lot." The sarcastic tone lashed out at her, and stung more than a physical blow ever could.

"While you were busy with Kyle, I called my boss. That lunch meeting was to inform me of his presence and the change of plans. However, since I brought you along instead of going out of the way to run you back to the house, she decided not to bring it up. She figured it was better to come from your handler than the person you just met, so she handed me the manila envelope. We were so busy with the other appointments that I never opened it. When I called her, her response was that I should open the envelope, and that it would explain everything."

When he said nothing, she felt the need to fill the silence with the only thing she could think of. "What happened that day wasn't your fault."

"What do you know about it?"

"I read the official report." She kept her voice low, almost wishing she hadn't said anything. When his eyelids flew open and he looked at her, there was a mixture of horror and worry shining through the blue eyes she loved so much.

"You what? How did you get your hands on that?"

"Graves sent it, and it was in the envelope. You can't blame yourself for what happened."

"The hell I can't. We received that tip anonymously, and instead of waiting for back-up we went in. It got one of my men killed and injured Phillips beyond repair. His life will never be the same, neither will the family of the other man who died because of my screw-up." He closed his eyes again and shook his head. "That was the second mission after I had been promoted to Gunnery Sergeant."

"I know the cost was high, but in the end you took down the target. You saved lives by taking him down. That's not something that should be forgotten."

"What should never be forgotten are the ones killed in action, and the ones who've had their lives changed forever by the acts of war." He kept his eyes closed, but his body tensed up again. Was he thinking about all the blood spilled?

"People will never forget. You will never forget. It's never easy, but Lucky…" She reached out and took his hand. He remained stiff, but didn't pull away. "You can't blame yourself. Look at Kyle, he doesn't blame you. According to the information I found, he's married and happier than he's ever been."

He let out a huff of doubt but she pushed forward. "He met his wife when he returned stateside for his recovery. They married four months ago and are completely in love. You should be happy for him."

"The man lost two of his limbs because of my decision, and you want me to be happy for him?" The guilt tainted his words.

"I want you to be happy that he's alive, that he's living his life, and has love in it. He's not less of a man because he's missing limbs or has burns on his face and body." She took her hand away, and stood. "Look at how far he's come. Last time you saw him, you weren't sure he was going to live, and now he's living a life like everyone else. With the aid of prosthetic limbs, he's walking, driving, and doing everything else that people do. Why are you denying him that?"

"Denying him…" His eyes popped open, and the heat burned within his gaze. "You have no idea what you're talking about."

"I don't? Very well then. I'll let you sulk in private." She turned on her heels and headed for the door. "But I take back what I said before about making other arrangements. Get yourself together, because tomorrow afternoon the two of you will be interviewed together."

She continued down the hall to her bedroom. If he wanted to live in the nightmare of what had happened, then so be it. She couldn't pull him from his thoughts. Those were demons he'd have to fight himself. But she'd be damned if she was going to change the interview because he was too stubborn to see that his friend had moved past just being a wounded veteran and had begun to live again.

She pushed her door until it was halfway closed, just in case he came to his senses, and headed to the bathroom. She'd have a long, hot bath and try not to worry if she was doing the right thing. *So much for telling him I want to give us a second chance. If I don't get fired, my job is going to drive us apart.*

Lucky wasn't sure how long he was stretched out on the bed feeling sorry for himself, but when he finally sat up there was no doubt it was the middle of the night. The moon was high in the sky, and every house he could see was dark. He wasn't sure there would ever be a day that he didn't regret not giving the order to retreat earlier. Or the decision to go off the road in order to turn around. He was too eager to prove himself as a leader and catch the man they hunted. His mistake could have got every one of them killed.

He went to the bathroom and splashed cold water on his face. In the mirror, he caught a glimpse of himself, the pale skin with five o'clock stubble clearly showing. Around his eyes, he looked drawn and tired. The cool water helped to rejuvenate him, and he decided it was time to find Maddie. He owed her an apology. His behavior was unacceptable, and the only excuse he had was that he'd never dealt with what happened to Kyle before. He just stuffed it into a box deep within him and went on with his work.

After he dried his face, he had nothing else left to delay himself. "Here goes nothing," he mumbled to his reflection before heading toward the door.

Down the hall, he peeked into her room. The comforter and sheets were pulled back, but she wasn't there. The bathroom door that adjoined the room stood open, and the light was out, so he didn't bother to check to see if she was there. The only other place she'd be was downstairs. What was she doing up at this time of night?

He didn't bother to turn on the hall light as he descended the stairs. He saw a flicker of light. The warm orange glow told him it couldn't have been the television. Wondering what it was, he sped his pace.

There in the living room, she was sprawled out on the sofa with the gas fireplace going. He knew she wasn't asleep because she kept mumbling something he couldn't make out. "Umm, Maddie."

"Stop calling me that." She didn't even turn around to face him.

"I can't. You'll always be my Maddie." He came around to the side of the sofa. "What are you doing up? Is it because of me?"

"Do you always think you're to blame for everything?" She pulled her legs up, giving him room to sit, and curled on her side to face the fireplace. "You know, not everything is about you."

"I understand you're angry with me."

"You always think you know everything," she grumbled.

"Maybe just upset, then. But I came to apologize." He sat down in the spot she'd cleared for him. "Kyle was a shock, one I wasn't ready for. I don't blame you for being angry with me because of my rude comments."

"I'm not angry, I'm…" She paused and took a deep breath.

He leaned closer as the color drained from her face. "Are you okay?"

"I'm fine." She placed a hand on her stomach and closed her eyes.

"You don't look fine."

"Damn it, I said I was fine." After a few moments of silence, she opened her eyes. "I'm sorry, I shouldn't have snapped at you. As I was saying, I'm not angry. I just hate to see you beat yourself up over something you couldn't control. What happened on that mission isn't something you can just go back and fix. Some might call it our destiny." She held up her hand when he started to interrupt her. "Don't bitch at me. I'm just saying it led Kyle to his wife. Maybe that's worth something. I know it killed another of your Marines, and I'm sorry, but each of us have a destiny we're put here on this Earth for."

"So, his was to be killed in action?"

"Do you know his wife started a business in his honor?"

"What?" He had no idea what she was talking about.

"It's called Sewn with Love. Surely you've heard of them? They've been all over the news. She turns the uniforms and clothes into something special for military spouses. It started out as a way to remember those who were killed in action, but it's gone far beyond that. Any spouse or family member can send in their clothes and she will turn it into whatever they want. Quilts are the biggest thing, but she also does pillows, purses, and more."

"What does this have to do with what happened?"

"Cassy Weber has done something for his memory, and for the memories of others who have died during their service to our country. She's turning tragedy into something that's cherished. She gave her husband's life and his death meaning, and by doing that she's giving others closure. Maybe that was her destiny." She paused for a moment before letting a light sigh escape. "Maybe it sounds harsh, but I've met some of the people she's done this for. It's nothing to be taken lightly."

He looked at her for a moment and considered what she said before shaking his head. "I can't justify that a man was killed so his wife could make quilts. But this isn't the reason I came in here. What happened that day is in my mind. I could have ordered us to wait for the second Humvee, or ordered our retreat when I knew something was off, but I was determined to prove myself. Either way, I shouldn't have taken it out on you."

"You didn't."

He brought her hand to his lips, and kissed the top of her knuckles. "Seeing

Kyle was a shock. The last time I tried, he was still in the hospital and had refused to even look at me. I know he was angry at the world, but it only made me beat myself up harder over what happened. To see him today…well, it was a jolt to say the least. Then to learn he had pulled himself up by his bootstraps and put his life back together means everything. This woman he met must be someone special."

"Everyone deserves a special someone." She leaned toward him and cupped the palm of her hand to his cheek. "I tried to tell you earlier I want to see where this goes."

"Even after what you learned today?"

"Nothing I learned or will ever learn would change my mind. I ran away years ago because I didn't think we could handle the distance…actually, I didn't think I could. We were nearly inseparable, and I wasn't even sure I knew who I was when you weren't around. But times have changed, I've changed, and I want to see where things can go." She let her hand fall away and leaned back. "I don't expect you to step up and be a father to my baby. I just want you to know I don't expect anything from you."

"What do you mean?"

"I don't want you to think that I'm only willing to do this so my child has a father. I had already decided to raise him or her myself. So, that doesn't play into this decision."

He wasn't sure if he should be offended or not. He hadn't considered her wanting a father for the child as the reason for her to agree to explore things between them. However, if he was going to go down this road with her, he was going to be fully committed. That meant they'd have a few months to determine if things would work.

"Either we're in this completely or we're not. That means we're in *everything*. You can't just push me aside while you try to parent the child alone. If this is going to work, then you need to trust me. You didn't trust me or us all those years ago. Are you willing to do it this time? I want to be a part of your life, and this baby's life. The question is…will you let me?"

The silence stretched on for longer than he'd have liked. Long enough for doubts to rise within him, but it was the only way. No matter how much he loved her, he wouldn't be content in this relationship if he were kept out of such a big portion of her life. Depending on her answer, he might have just made himself a father. A bit of excitement blossomed within him. He wanted Maddie and this baby with him.

She tucked a strand of hair behind her ear. "I trust you and I want this to work."

He leaned forward and pressed his lips to hers. The sweetness of her mint lip gloss made him want more. He rose up on his knees and cupped the back of her head. With a gentle nudge, she opened up to him, and he slipped his tongue between her lips.

Oh, how he'd missed her.

Chapter Eight

The following week had gone by quicker than Lucky had expected. Even the media interviews had been less of a pain than he'd thought they would be. Once he got past talking about himself and what inspired him to cook, it was easier. Then again, maybe it was his new outlook, or the weightlessness to his step, now that he had Maddie back in his life. Love did funny things to men, and he was not immune to it.

Recipes had been tested over and over again, but he had yet to settle on what to make for the judges. He only had a week left to decide, yet that was the last thing on his mind. Things had begun to progress with Maddie. Each day he had worked to make sure she could see they were meant to be together. They had a week left, and he was going to convince her things could work between them.

"Lucky?"

Her heels clicked on the hardwood floors, and he turned to see her just as she stepped out of her office. Strands of hair slipped out of the bun and fell down around her face. Jeans and a spaghetti strap tank top hugged her curves, showing off the slight baby bump, making her look completely breathtaking. "Huh?"

"Why are you looking at me like that?" As if his gaze made her self-conscious, she wrapped her arms around her body.

"Don't." He set down the tongs he'd used to flip the sausage, which was part of his homemade pasta sauce with peppers and onions for tomorrow's lunch with one of the reporters from a big magazine. The timing for the interview was perfect, and it would make a big impression. *Guess Maddie's still hoping I'll win, and maybe I will…just so I can spend an additional two weeks with her.*

He stalked toward her, and every step he took surged his desire to pick her up and carry her upstairs. "Don't hide yourself from me. Don't let your self-consciousness overwhelm you. To me, every inch of you is beautiful. If I could have my way, we'd spend all our free time naked and in bed, making up for lost time."

"Lucky…I'm…"

"I know, my sweet Maddie, you're not ready. I promised I wouldn't push, and I haven't, but I won't let you hide the little pleasures you give me." He caressed her hips, running his hand along her waist, and watched as the simple touch hardened her nipples until they stood out like small beads under her shirt. "Your body reacts to me."

"It always has." She brought her hand up to his cheek. "It's sad to think we're halfway through our time together. Then…who knows."

"I know I'm not letting you go like last time." He wrapped his arms around her waist and pulled her close. "I want you to come back to Virginia with me."

"My job is in D.C. but it's only a few hours away. Maybe we can still make this work…even with the distance."

He had thought about how he'd convince her to move to Virginia with him, but all of a sudden his plans slipped away. "Could you find another job to be close to me?" He raised an eyebrow at her, but before she could answer, he grew serious. "You need to be around family and friends. Raising a child is a lot of work. You need a strong support system."

"I…"

"There are plenty of young children among us…" He placed his hand on the small bump of her stomach. "This little girl or boy will be surrounded by love. Roulette, Wynn's daughter, and the Garcia twins."

"You make it sound easy. Like we can just pick up where we left off. That not a single thing has changed."

"Things have changed, but there's no reason we can't be together. I don't want to miss a single day with you. Come back to Virginia with me. Let's take this second chance, and not let another moment slip by."

"I don't know." She bit the corner of her bottom lip.

He slipped his hand from her stomach, clasping both hands around the small of her back, bringing her closer to him. "You don't have to give me an answer yet, but think about it." When she nodded, he added, "If I could, I'd pick up and move to be with you. I'd do whatever it takes, but even if it's possible, it will take some time. My contract isn't up for another two years…"

"I'm not asking you to give up the Marines. You've worked hard to be where you are, and you love it." She teased her fingers along his collar, barely brushing against the skin. "I can't see you enjoying civilian life much."

"I know you're not asking, but I would do it if it meant being with you. I love you, Maddie. Always have and I always will."

"I love you, too. Just give me some time to think about it."

The sizzling of the sausage brought his thoughts back to the stove, but did nothing to calm the fires burning within him. "Are you done with the phone calls you had to make?"

"Yeah, do you need some help?"

"No, but you're more than welcome to keep me company. The sausage is nearly done for tomorrow, but I won't make the sauce until morning. It's better fresh. I'm going to start preparing for dinner."

"I think it's great you're having Kyle over for dinner before he leaves tomorrow. I was worried things would be tense for you in those interviews, but you breezed right through. You and Kyle made a good team and kept each of the interviews interesting."

"Since he's been here, I've gotten a chance to see that he's accepted what happened and has moved on with his life. I'm happy for him and his wife. I promised that once this was all over, I'd visit Kentucky where they bought a little horse farm. I still can't picture him on a horse farm, but he says he loves it. It's something I've got to see." He stepped away from her and back to the stove. "Maybe you'll join me. We'll make it before the baby's due, and we can even have a few days to ourselves without all this competition going on."

"You'll have two or four weeks off, won't you have to get back?"

"I think I can get Graves to agree to a few extra days *if* I win." He pulled the skillet off the burner and set it aside to cool before he broke it down for the sauce.

"Even more incentive to win. You're going to give it your all, then?"

"Would you expect anything less from me?" He shot her a quick smirk before opening the refrigerator, grabbing what he needed to get dinner started. "Just the extra two weeks with you is worth it. But when you add in the money for the wounded Marines, and doing this for Kyle, how can I not? I'll give it everything I've got and then some."

"That's a change." She leaned against the counter, plucked a banana from the basket, and pealed back the skin.

The duck breast he had just pulled out of the refrigerator nearly fell out of his hand as he watched her take such care with the banana. She pulled back the skin, and as the tip slid between her lips, he thought he'd lose his self-control then and there. Even though she wasn't trying to be sexual, she was, and it was turning him on. "Maddie." Her name came out as more of a growl than he'd meant it to.

"Hmmm."

"Damn, woman, you keep that up and I won't be responsible for my actions."

She took another bite before the realization dawned on her. "Oh."

"You make me feel like a teenager again with only one thing on the brain."

"Maybe I should go get ready? I don't want to distract you."

"I like being distracted by you." He went to her, his body tight against hers, while keeping her locked between him and the counter. "You're all I think about. Not just in a sexual way. I want you in every way. I want what we had, and slowly we're getting it back, but I don't want our time to come to an end."

"Same here. But let's just get through this, and we'll see what happens." She tipped her head back to look up at him. "If you don't need me, I'll go get ready. Kyle will be here in an hour."

"Is that a distraction to keep me from throwing you over my shoulder and carrying you upstairs?"

"No, but you'd regret it later if you mess things up on the last night with him in town." She placed her hand on his chest. "There's plenty of time. I'm not going anywhere. I promise."

"I'd go UA to follow you and bring you back if I had to." Even as he said the words, he knew it was true. Never before would he have considered something so dire, but he wasn't going to lose her this time. No matter what it cost him.

Showered and dressed, Madison sat on the cedar chest at the foot of the bed. Her thoughts were going a hundred miles per hour as she considered all that had happened in the past week. It seemed like it had gone by in a blur, the fastest being the moments she was alone with Lucky. She wanted to throw caution to the wind, give up her job, and move to be with Lucky. Public relations managers were always in demand, and no matter where she lived, she could find work.

She might like her condo and job in Washington D.C., but she loved Lucky. That was more important. But one week wasn't enough time to know things would work. They both had changed over the years, and no matter what they felt, it didn't mean things would go smoothly.

With a baby on the way, she needed a solid foundation, and that meant a career that would provide for her and her child. Her employers knew she was pregnant, and while the timing wasn't the best, they'd make it work. Finding a job while pregnant might be harder. She didn't care that it was illegal to discriminate, because she knew people still did it, and her pregnancy would be considered when they were hiring.

"Darling, we're going to be just fine." She ran a hand over her stomach and glanced in the mirror. The baby bump was still small, but it was a clear announcement that she was going to be a mother in just a few months. "I can't wait to meet you."

In two weeks, she had an appointment with her OBGYN for an ultrasound, and if the baby were in the right position, she'd be able to learn the sex. "Little one, I'd appreciate you cooperating. I've got shopping to do before I'm too big to move around the store."

"You'll be beautiful." Lucky stood in the doorway.

"What?"

"You'll be beautiful through your whole pregnancy. There's a glow to you, even when you're looking a little green from morning sickness."

"I'll never understand why they call it morning sickness when it lasts all day." She rose from the chest and looked at herself in the mirror one last time to make sure everything was perfect. The sky blue dress was a little snug around her waist, but flowed nicely and ended an inch above her knee. Her make-up was just as she had applied it, but even she could see the slight paleness beneath. "I'm ready. Are you sure you don't want me to go out, and you two can spend tonight catching up?"

"I want you by my side, tonight and always." He strolled toward her and took her hand into his. "You look gorgeous."

The doorbell rang before she could gather a reply. There was something about him that left her grasping for words. He was a man of action, but his words always sent her heart fluttering. The man she'd always wanted to spend her life with—but decisions had divided them. "Go ahead down. I'll be there in a minute."

With a brief nod, he headed downstairs to the door, leaving her alone once again. Her memories turned to a night very similar to tonight. But instead of Kyle, it had been Ace and Wynn joining them for dinner.

Lucky had spent most of the afternoon cooking what was supposed to be a romantic dinner for two, but when she arrived at the Diamond household she found Lucky in less than a romantic mood. "What's wrong? Dinner not coming along as planned? Anything I can do?"

He pulled out a pot from the oven before turning toward her. "Dinner's fine, it's just the company I'm disappointed with."

"Hmm, shall I take offense to that?" She tipped her head to the living room where two other Diamonds were waiting. "Or shall I assume you mean them?"

"Them?" The lid clanked against the roaster as he checked dinner. "Everything was perfect until Mom came home. She's grounded Wynn, so we're stuck with her. Ace got back for the weekend on leave, and he's too exhausted to move. He's refusing to go out. So, I guess that means we're stuck with him as well."

"It's okay. We'll have dinner together, and then maybe we can spend some time alone. Ace will go to bed and you can order Wynn upstairs to study or something. What about your parents, are they joining us, too?" She didn't care that Ace and Wynn were around. After all, Wynn was her best friend and she liked Ace, but she had hoped for a quieter evening with Lucky.

"No, they're out for the evening and won't be back until late. That's why I thought we'd

have dinner here instead of going out. Wynn said she had plans, and I hadn't expected Ace to be home."

"It's okay. I'm not upset. Plus, it will be nice to see Ace. It's been months since he's been home."

That night was their graduation celebration. The next morning, they'd graduate and it would start their countdown to him shipping off and her starting college. Wynn would have one year left in high school. Gwen had already headed off to college the year before. All three of the friends would be separated.

As the memory fell away, it left traces of how scared she'd been to go off to college by herself. She had been so close to Gwen and Wynn in high school, even though they'd been in different grades. Back then, things like that had a way of dividing friendships. Even through it all, theirs had remained strong.

"I wish I could go back to that time, where everything was so much simpler, and all of us were together."

 # Chapter Nine

Dinner had gone smoothly and Lucky had even enjoyed the time reminiscing with Kyle, but he was anxious to get Maddie alone again. Something had seemed to be bothering her since she had joined them downstairs, but anytime he had a second alone with her to ask, she brushed him off as if it was nothing.

"So, Kyle, what made you buy a horse farm?" Maddie sat on the far end of the sofa, a mug of hot tea in hand.

"My wife, Staci, was raised on a horse farm. Her parents didn't own it, but after his service her father trained horses, taught her everything she knows, and her mother was a veterinarian. It's the one thing she's always wanted. Since I needed something to devote my time to, I decided to give it a shot. We moved to Kentucky, bought the farm, and haven't looked back since." He paused and took a long swig from his beer. "We breed, train, and even race our mustangs. We have a few horses that are boarded on the farm as well."

"My mother always loved horses, and when I was young she signed me up for a riding class. I enjoyed it but haven't been on one since."

"You're more than welcome to come when Lucky visits, and we can rectify that."

"Don't think you're getting me on a horse." Lucky shook his head. "Not my thing. I'll watch you."

"That's what I said to Staci when she first told me about wanting to own a horse farm." Kyle gave her a wink. "She got me on one, and I think Maddie can do the same for you."

"I don't know about that."

"Well, I let you two love birds work that out." He stood and grabbed his beer bottle. "I should be going. As much as I've enjoyed this trip, and seeing you again, I'm looking forward to getting back to Staci."

"It was great seeing you." Lucky stood and took the bottle from the other man. "I mean that. And I will take you up on your offer to come to Kentucky. I'm looking forward to meeting Staci."

"You'd better. She was disappointed she couldn't make the journey out to meet you, but we've got a horse due any day now, and it's been a rough pregnancy. Staci didn't want to leave her in case things went south. Our first mare. She's attached." Before he headed for the door, he turned back to her. "I look forward to seeing you again. Until then, you take care of him."

"Oh, I will, and I'm going to make sure he wins."

"I've no doubt." Kyle cupped a hand over Lucky's shoulder. "Give them hell, like you've always given the men, and I know you'll come out on top."

"I'll win this for you." Lucky nodded.

"Not just for me, but for all of the Marines."

He followed Kyle to the door to show him out. There was no doubt that each of the contestants wanted to win this for their branch, but his duty to bring home the prize was strong because of Kyle. He'd only known him a few months before the mission that left him wounded, yet they had grown quite close over the last few days. He'd win this for him, and all the other wounded veterans who needed that money.

Lost in her own thoughts, she moved around the kitchen cleaning up the last bits from dinner, placing their dishes in the dishwasher, and wiping down the counter. The evening had gone off just as Lucky had planned, and the conversation had been easy, but her thoughts had been jumbled most of the night. She hadn't even heard Lucky as he returned.

"I'd have done that."

"I just wiped off the counter and added the last few items to the dishwasher." She rung out the rag and draped it over the spigot. "If you'll excuse me, I need to return a couple phone calls that came through while we were having dinner." She hated to lie, but she didn't want to divulge who she was really calling, or even what was on her mind.

"You've been distant tonight. Is everything okay?"

"Oh, yeah, fine." She tried to keep her tone light, but she knew she was failing.

"Well, whenever you're ready to talk about it, you know where to find me. Meanwhile, I'm going to shower."

Not knowing what else to say, she nodded. "Goodnight."

She stood there by the kitchen counter and waited until she heard the water for the shower start. Then she let out the deep breath she'd been holding and snatched her cell phone from the counter. The hour was a little later than she had wanted, but she needed to talk to someone. After the fourth ring, she was ready to hang up when Gwen's sleepy voice finally answered.

"Sorry to wake you." She slipped into the office and shut the door, so that once Lucky finished in the shower, he wouldn't be able to hear her.

"Madison, is that you? Is everything okay?"

"Yeah, I'm sorry. I know you're probably exhausted, but I need a friend." Guilt stabbed through her heart at knowing she was one of the reasons Gwen would be tired the next day. It was selfish, but she needed someone to confide in.

"You know I'm always here for you. What's up?" Gwen was a little more awake now.

"I'm falling back in love with Lucky." She blurted it out before she could rein herself in. "I mean…I never stopped loving him, but being so close to him this past week makes me want to make up for all our lost time."

"Forgive me. It might be the mommy brain, but I don't understand what the problem is. So…you love him, and want to make up for lost time. Do it. I mean, unless there's another man you're hiding somewhere. What's the problem?"

Madison was already neck deep, so she might as well take the full plunge. "I'm pregnant."

"Wait, what? It can't be…*his*."

The way she said *his* made Madison wonder if Ace had just woken up, but it didn't matter because he'd find out sooner or later. Most likely after the phone call. "No, I'm just over eighteen weeks pregnant, so it's not Lucky's. It's a long story, and I'll tell you someday, but this only complicates things further."

"Does he know?"

"Yes to both parts. Like I've said, things have happened this week, and although we haven't fallen into bed or anything like that, it's clear we are in love with each other. He also knows I'm pregnant because I told him a few nights ago."

"And?" All the sleep was gone from Gwen's voice.

"What do you mean *and*? I'm pregnant with another man's child, yet I'm thinking about picking up with an ex. It's complicated." She suddenly wished she had called Wynn instead, especially since she knew Gwen's own story. "Plus, it means giving up my job, moving to Virginia. It's all bad timing."

"When you told Lucky you were pregnant, did he tell you about Roulette, that Ace isn't her biological father?"

"Yes, but this is different."

"I don't see how." Gwen stated as if it was clear. "You saw Ace with *our* daughter." She stressed the *our* part to make sure Madison understood.

"I did." Images of the two of them together flashed before her eyes. "But it's a complete change of lifestyle. What will I do for work? I've got to be able to provide for my child."

"Public relations is always in demand so I know you can find something." Gwen shuffled the phone and it sounded like she'd readjusted in bed before coming back on the line. "Do you love him enough to change your life for him…if it means spending the rest of your life with him?"

"Yes." There was no hesitation. She'd give up everything to be with him. To have what Gwen and Ace had.

"Then the answer is simple." A baby cried in the background, announcing the end of their conversation. "I've got to go. Madison, I'm happy for you. Don't let this chance pass you by. Grab him, and hold on tight. Love's a ride you won't forget, full of ups and downs, but having him on that journey with you will make it all worth it."

After she'd hung up, she sat there and considered things. She was tired of overthinking the situation. If he was willing to be with her even though she was pregnant with another man's child, why should she doubt it? He had always told her that their love was strong, that they'd be able to get through anything. She didn't believe him years ago, but now she did. They were worth fighting for.

Instead of feeling sorry for herself, she decided to go to him. With each step, her confidence grew, until finally she reached the top of the stairs. His door was open but the lights were off. Even that didn't stop her from going inside.

"Lucky?" She whispered from the doorway, not wanting to wake him if he had fallen asleep after his shower.

"I'm up." He didn't bother to turn on a light. "I just got into bed, but if you need me to come downstairs, give me a minute and I'll get dressed."

"No. Umm, can I come in?"

"Sure."

He leaned up against the headboard, and the rays of moonlight streaked in the window, illuminating his body. He was so much more physically fit than he'd been in high school. He was more toned than he'd been back then, making her want to run her fingers along his chest to feel the differences.

"I love you." As she moved farther into his room, the view of him shirtless had her nervous. Everything she had considered before she stepped through the doorway had suddenly disappeared from her thoughts.

"I love you, too, Maddie, but are you okay? You seem off tonight."

"I was off because I was considering what was happening between us. I've decided something…"

"Come here." He held out his hand to her, and when she went to him, he nodded. "Go on; tell me what's on your mind."

"I'll come back to Virginia if you still want me. I'll travel anywhere…if it means being with you."

"How could I not want you there with me?" He pulled back the covers. He smirked at her when she glanced under the blanket to make sure he had something on. "Don't worry, I've got shorts on. Come here. Just let me hold you."

Without hesitation, she slipped onto the bed beside him. "Tomorrow I'll put in my three week notice."

"Three weeks?"

"Whether you win or not, I have to see this competition through. That means those additional two weeks with the winner. If it's you, then that's wonderful. If not, I'll join you in Virginia two weeks after that. Well, maybe three weeks. I'll have to return to D.C. to sort out my office and condo, pack my stuff. Plus, I have a doctor's appointment."

"We'll work everything out. D.C. isn't that far from Virginia Beach, so we can get your stuff down there when I'm not on duty. As for your condo, what about renting it out? There's always a demand for places there."

"Yeah, I was thinking that. I have a friend who's a real estate agent who can handle it. I'll rent it furnished, and then I won't have to deal with any of it."

He ran a hand down her arm. "We haven't actually discussed it, but I'd like you to move in with me. Not just down to Virginia Beach. My condo is two bedrooms, so if you don't want to sleep with me you can always have that room. But I want you with me. I want to come home every day and see you there."

"Every time I agree with you on something, you want to take it one step further." She turned toward him, pressing the front of her body against the side of his. "You're never satisfied, Lucky Diamond."

"I'll be satisfied when you agree to marry me."

Marriage? His expression announced that he was completely serious, and she had to swallow the lump that had formed in her throat before she could speak. "Is that a proposal? Because you're going to need to do better than that if you want me as your wife."

"Maddie, I know you, and I know you're not ready to say yes. I'm going to wear you down, and sometime soon you *will* say yes."

"You're so confident." She tried to relax her body, but every muscle within her seemed to have a mind of its own and stayed rigid.

"I am, and I plan to have you as my wife before the baby is born. That gives me just over four months."

The very thought stirred excitement and nervousness within her. He was right on one thing. She wasn't ready to agree to marriage. A week wasn't enough time to determine if they were still compatible, let alone if they were still in love. The feelings he stirred within her might just be left over from what they had once shared. Even as she thought it, she doubted it. If she knew one thing, she knew she loved him with everything that was in her. But was love enough?

Morning came with the blaring ringtone of a cell phone. Thinking it was hers, Madison cursed as she rolled over to grab it off the nightstand, slamming straight into Lucky. "What? Oh, hell!" She didn't have time to consider things further as she realized it was his phone going off and not hers.

He brought it to his ear without even checking the caller ID. "Hello?"

As she began to wake up, her memories of how she'd ended up in bed with him returned. They had talked until she began to doze off. She couldn't remember what he'd said, but he had convinced her to stay curled up against him and sleep.

"Hold on, she's right here." He pulled the phone away from his ear and held it out to her. "It's Wynn. She wants to talk to you."

"Me?"

"Take it before I verbally tear her limb to limb for spoiling my perfect morning. One I've dreamed of all these years. Instead of waking up and snuggling with you, I'm woken up by the phone."

Relenting, she took the phone. "Hello."

"Madison, it's Wynn. I spoke to Gwen this morning and planned to call you, but I forgot to get your cell phone number from her. Since I'm already down at the store, I thought I'd call Lucky."

"I thought you weren't working much at the shops, just designing?"

"I am, but that's not why I called. One sec." Wynn mumbled something to someone on the other end before coming back to the phone. "Sorry about that. Anyway, I wanted to talk to you right away. I've got a solution to your problems."

She glanced at Lucky. "Umm, I think it's okay now."

"Oh, so you aren't moving here?" The disappointment was clear in Wynn's voice.

"I am." She curled back into his embrace. "Word travels faster than a speeding bullet, apparently. I just spoke to Gwen a few hours ago."

"Gwen?" Lucky questioned.

"Quiet, I'll tell you later."

"Did I interrupt something?" Wynn sounded embarrassed. "If so, I really don't want to know what you and my brother are doing."

"Actually, we're just cuddling in bed. There's nothing wrong with that. He also knows I'm moving there. I told him last night, which is how I ended up in bed with him."

"Seriously, I don't need to know." Wynn's voice was higher than normal. "My two best friends and my brothers, it makes me want to say *yuck* and spit out my tongue. Whatever the two of you see in them, I'll never understand. They put me through hell growing up, but I still love them."

"Wynn, was there a reason you called at the crack of dawn?"

"To offer you a job."

"What?" She eyed Lucky, but he couldn't have known about this since he had been snuggling with her all night.

"My husband, Boom, and I have been discussing this for a while. I've wanted to bring on a public relations expert to handle the marketing for Roll of the Diamond and Heart of a Diamond. Who better than you?"

"What do I know about marketing clothes?"

"More than I do." Wynn laughed. "I just wanted to design them, which is why I opened my own store. Then New York came to me, and things have been crazy ever since. I need some help, and I want it to be you. We can learn together, and more importantly we'll all be together again. Come on, what do you say?"

"I've already agreed to come there. As for a job…can I have time to think about it?" She was truly honored, but with all the changes happening so quickly, she didn't want to jump in with both feet before considering it.

"Sure. I'm going to email my marketing plans and some other information to Lucky's email account and you can look over them. I'll include all the details of the job, and if there's anything you want to change, just let me know. This is a learning curve for me as well. But I want you on this project with me."

"Okay, I'll look over them this evening. I'll let you know within the next forty-eight hours. Umm, Wynn…did Gwen tell you I'm pregnant?"

"Yes and congratulations."

"No, I mean…I understand if you want someone else for the job."

"Don't be silly. I wouldn't have asked if I didn't want you. As far as I'm concerned, there's no one better." There was a man's voice in the background, before Wynn spoke again. "Boom just arrived. We're off to find paint for the nursery, so I've got to go but I can't wait to see you."

"Okay. Have fun. I'll be in touch." She hit the end button, and let her head fall back against the pillows.

"What's this about a job?"

"Wynn is nuts." She chuckled. "She wants me to come and work for her as the public relations manager. I guess she spoke with Gwen this morning and found out I was considering moving back home to be with you."

"So, are you going to take it?"

"She's sending all the information to your email. If you could forward it to me, I can consider things further this afternoon. But…maybe. It sounds like it could be interesting."

He rolled to his side and propped himself up on his elbows. "There's something else I should tell you."

"Hmm?" She let her eyelids fall shut so she could enjoy the moment in his arms.

"When your parents wanted to move to Florida, I bought your old family home. Before you bitch about it, they didn't tell you because I asked them not to."

"But why? Why did you buy it?"

"Because I wanted it. You loved that house, and I thought someday you'd come back to me. I thought we might move in and raise our own family there."

"What about all these years? You had to have figured I wasn't coming back." She remembered how much she'd loved the house she grew up in, and how devastated she was when she found out her parents had sold it. She hadn't even gotten one final visit home before they closed the deal. No one had told her they were even thinking about it until after the sale was complete.

"I admit I lost hope that we might ever be together again, but I couldn't see someone else owning that home. It meant so much to you, and therefore it meant a lot to me. I've kept it, but I couldn't bring myself to live there. Not without you. I've rented it out. Currently, I have it rented to a family that had lived on base but wanted to have a place of their own. They just received notice they'll be moving. Before you showed up in Graves's office, I had considered selling it, but now that you're here, I want us to move in there. We can raise our child there, and when I'm deployed Ace and Gwen will be right around the corner."

"Raise this child in my old home…" Tears swam in her eyes. "Oh, Lucky, I can't believe you."

"Is that a yes?"

"But what about your condo? Ace said you love that place."

"I do, but I'd rather be in a house where our child can run around, play in the creek, visit their aunt, uncle, and cousin just over the creek. We can make that a home for our family."

"Your determination is showing through again." She smirked. "Let's do it."

"Another one down, only one more to go. Next up to bat…marriage."

She swatted at his chest, but he caught her hand before she could make contact. "We'll see about that."

 # Epilogue

Lucky's part of the competition was over. Now they just had to wait. Sergeant Major Graves had called that morning to wish him the best. It had been the first time they'd spoken since Lucky had been called into his office and given his new orders. It had also been the first chance he had to ask why he hadn't been told that Kyle had been the one who recommended him.

I didn't want it to put you off your game. Seeing Phillips was better than me telling you. It was his recommendation, so he needed to be the one to explain why. The words played in his thoughts again, and even though he had the answer, he didn't care.

Maddie ran her hand along his thigh as she did her best to distract him, but nothing could keep his mind from what the judges were doing now. He had been the first contestant to cook for the judges, and the hours since had gone by at a snail's pace.

"This is the first time in weeks we don't have an interview, and you don't need to spend the evening cooking or testing new recipes. Why don't we take advantage of it? Maybe we should go out and celebrate my new employment."

"I still can't believe Wynn talked you into taking on the public relations for her designs. Before you know it, she's going to be global."

"I can't believe it either." Excitement laced her voice, and she couldn't keep the smile from curling up the corners of her lips. The future would be nothing like her yesterdays, and for that she was thrilled. Challenges were what she enjoyed, and her new adventure would be full of them. "I just hope I can do the job the way she wants. Marketing clothes is very different then my previous experience. Especially since so many of her designs are aimed at military families. The patriotic line is amazing, but I'll need specialized marketing to highlight it. I've got some ideas, but I need to give it some additional thought."

"I've no doubt that you'll be amazing at it." He ran his hand along her body. "Though I won't deny that I'm excited that you found something because it means you'll be in Virginia with me."

"Come on, Lucky." She rubbed his shoulder. "You're too uptight. Whatever is going to happen will happen. You need to relax."

"How am I supposed to keep my mind off what's coming next? If I don't win, I'm plane bound for Virginia tomorrow, and you're off on a whirlwind of two more weeks of commitments. If that happens, it's going to be the longest two weeks since boot camp."

"We'll get through it." She curled against his body on the sofa. "Then, when it's over, we'll be together."

"I'm not letting you get away from me again." He kissed the top of her head. "Actually, I think it's time."

"Time for what?"

In answer, he got down on one knee in front of her. He gave her a moment to realize what he was about to ask her. "Maddie, I fell in love with you when you first came splashing around our creek. Your reddish brown curls flying in the breeze and your carefree personality won me over. The brief moments when you're mad and your temper flares allow me to see a different side of you. One that's just as fiery as your carefree side. It gives you the nickname I'll forever call you by. My Maddie, I want you as my wife. You're my other half, the one I want to spend the rest of my life with and grow old with. I love you with everything in me. Will you marry me?"

"You told me you'd wait until I was ready, and until just now I wasn't sure what I would do when the time came. Now I know. This is all happening so fast. But…it's true that first loves are the hardest to get over, and I was never able to get over you. You've always been there with me, even when I was trying to deny it. I've always loved you. You're my world and if you can accept me and my child, then yes, I'll marry you."

"*Our* child," he corrected, as he pulled a ring out of his pocket and slipped it onto her finger.

"Our child." She looked down at her finger. The beautiful gold band with a large diamond in the middle and two smaller ones on either side shined up at her. "It's beautiful, but where did you get it?"

"I had Ace overnight it to me a few days ago. It's the ring I bought after graduation. I had planned to propose to you that morning at the bed and breakfast. I was going to set things up with a dozen red roses…" He moved back up on the sofa. "It doesn't matter. What matters is we've found each other again."

"The breakfast with the roses arrived while I was getting dressed."

"What?"

She stared down at the ring, which was now on her finger. "At the bed and breakfast…after you left, it came. I cried as I stared down at the perfect roses, the reds and whites mixed together just like I love, and the baby's breath. That's when the doubt hit me full force. I ran to the window just as you slammed the door on your truck and drove away."

"Maddie, that's the past. We've found each other again."

She reached up and cupped his cheek. "We have, but we've missed so much time we should have had together. We suffered years of heartache. I was scared we'd grow apart because of the physical separation."

"We don't know what would have happened." He placed his hand over hers. "We might have. You might have been right."

She shook her head, tears running down her cheeks. "Not us. We were in love, and we'd have gotten through it because we knew what we had was worth it."

"Now we'll have to make up for the time we lost." He rose from kneeling before her, and pulled her up to stand with him. "So, once this is all over, I'll get a few days of leave and we'll go to Kentucky. We'll see Kyle and Staci. We'll spend quality time cherishing the love we have for each other."

"That sounds like fun. I know I'm really looking forward to spending some time alone with you when this is all over. No running to interviews, or photo shots. Just time with you."

He wrapped his arms around her waist. "Then I want us to move into your old house. I want to make a home for us and our child. And when you're ready, we'll set a wedding date. If you want to wait until the baby is born, we can. Whatever you want, because I just want you to be happy."

"Who'd have thought in just two short weeks my life would have changed this much, and I'd be marrying you. Life has been a whirlwind lately, but it led me to you." She leaned toward him and pressed her lips to his in a soft kiss. "I love you."

Her phone vibrated with a text message from her boss. *Gunnery Sergeant Diamond won, so I'm sure you wish to share the news with him. Congratulations. We'll see you in New York the day after tomorrow.*

"Oh, Lucky!" Tears spilled down her face as she held out the phone to him. "You did it."

He pulled her into his body and kissed her with more eagerness than before. It was time to celebrate their engagement and winning the competition.

Preview: Back from Hell

Marine for You Book Two

Lance Corporal Kyle Phillips's life has been blown apart by an IED explosion. All the work he put in at boot camp is worthless. Now he feels he's half the man he was before, with nothing to offer. His life fell apart in one brief moment and everything he worked for was gone. Better men than him died that day, and now he must come to terms with being chosen to live.

Staci Pence volunteers at a Veterans Affairs hospital in hopes that she could do something good. She had seen what the war had done to her father and in the end, he had taken his own life. Now she is using her own grief to save others. Her newest patient is Lance Corporal Phillips and while he believes he's damaged goods, not worthy of living, she's determined to show him otherwise.

Kyle had gotten to the point that he wished he'd died on that battlefield instead of living the life of half a man. That was until a woman with whiskey brown eyes and a feisty side strolled into his room looking to save him. Can he make peace with what has happened and open himself to the love Staci offers?

PART ONE

Chapter One

Kyle Phillips lay in a hospital bed with his eyes closed so he didn't have to look at what had become of his body. If he stayed that way, he could try to forget he'd lost a leg and arm in that IED explosion, leaving him half the man he was before. The burns along half of his body proved harder to forget. The pain down his side would not be denied.

Surgery after surgery helped to repair the damage left behind. That torturous experience had only done so much in returning him to the man he was before. There would always be scars along his face and body. Too many times he heard he should be thankful he was alive, while all the time he wished he had died overseas. It would have been better than living as a freak.

Gunnery Sergeant Lucky Diamond had left after Kyle refused to acknowledge the man who had been in charge of the fateful mission that left him so disfigured. How could he look his Gunnery Sergeant in the eyes, when he had failed? He was the one that handed the information to his Gunny and it not only left him in this state but had also gotten Weber killed.

Weber. A tear rolled down his cheek for his brother in arms. They graduated boot camp together and this had been their first deployment. A deployment that Weber never came back from. If either of them had known, would they have decided to do something besides join the military once they graduated high school? Or would the fact they did ultimately bring down their target outweigh the loss they had encountered? Gunnery Sergeant Diamond might blame himself, but it was nothing like the guilt Kyle carried.

He'd carry that guilt for the rest of his days, but it wouldn't change anything. He'd lost his friend and that hurt more than his own disfigurement. He and Weber had bonded over their training, encouraging each other through the worst parts, and now, when he needed his friend the most, he wasn't here. The loss pained him more than the loss of his limbs.

"I'd rather be where you are, Weber."

"Need something, Private First Class Phillips?" Brenda, the older day nurse, stood in his doorway. "I heard you talking to yourself. We have people who are paid to listen. Shall I get someone for you? Talking to thin air doesn't help much."

"No, thanks. I'm fine. Unless you can get me a bottle of whiskey."

"You know the rules. If you start working with your physical therapist, you'll be out of here in no time."

He tipped his head to the side and glared at her. Even with the anger, it was hard to be mad at someone who looked so much like someone's grandmother. All he wanted to do was get out of this place, but he wouldn't be able to do that until he learned to walk with his damn prosthesis and use the prosthetic arm. Physical therapy was the last thing he wanted. Every time he did those damn things, he was reminded he would never be whole again. The prosthesis might make him appear more normal, especially when he had long sleeves and pants, but all it did was hide reality.

When he lay in bed, he could keep his eyes closed and, with the phantom pains, it was almost as if he still had his limbs. The pains might be agonizing but, in those brief moments, he could pretend he was whole. Yet, the minute he opened his eyes, there was no more pretending. Nothing could hide the way the sheets fell flat just below the knee, or the fact his arm was gone from just below the elbow. His doctors tried to reassure him that, with the aid of his prosthesis, he could live a normal life. *Normal life.* Who would want to spend the rest of their life with a man who couldn't even hold them without the aid of some manmade arm?

"Remember we're only here to help. We want to see you regain your life."

Her words brought him back out of his thoughts for a moment and he watched her continue down the hallway. If they wanted to help him, they should just let him die. *Damn it Gunny, you should have let me die.* His earlier words rang through his thoughts. Even after the pain in Gunnery Sergeant Diamond's eyes, Kyle still didn't regret them. He wished he were dead rather than have to deal with this. He wasn't sure how to face the world again. Or even what to do with his life now. *What do I have to offer to anyone anymore?*

He glanced around the room and the need to get out of there rose within him. He didn't know where he'd go. He'd need aftercare and, as a foster child, he had no family to fall back on. His last foster family sent occasional letters to him but there was no chance he could stay with them while he figured out what to do with his life. Even his girlfriend of over two years had abandoned him. She couldn't deal with how he looked now.

"How did I miss how shallow she was?" The answer was as clear as his missing limbs. He'd overlooked it because he didn't want to see the truth. He wanted to enjoy the time they had together instead of thinking about their fights every time he put his military service before her. The biggest fight had happened just hours before he deployed. She wanted a serviceman on her arm because of *how good they looked in uniform*, her words, but she didn't want to deal with everything else that came along with it. He was naïve to think that with time she could overcome her issues and support him.

Alone and on the brink of a new life that he didn't want, he was ready to end it all. It might have been the easy way out but he didn't have the strength needed to endure the future days. A lone ship lost in the middle of darkness, no one would mourn for him. He wouldn't be missed.

He closed his eyes and he could almost hear his drill instructor hollering at him. *Get up, Marine! There's no quit in a Marine.*

Staci Pence dropped her bag behind the nurses' desk and prepared to do her rounds on the ward to see who might be interested in talking with her. Twice a week she came to the hospital to meet with service members who needed someone to confide in, or just a friendly little chat. Sometimes it was easier to talk to someone who was there as a friend than it was to talk to a counselor.

She had seen the cost of war in her father's eyes. Now, in his memory, she did whatever she could to give back. One last semester and then she hoped to get a job at the hospital as a physical therapist. That would lead her to her ultimate dream of owning a horse ranch. She enjoyed being a physical therapist and maybe, somehow, she could still manage to do it, although the horse ranch was deeply engrained in her veins. *One step at a time and you'll reach your dreams.*

"Staci, I've got someone I'd like you to visit." Brenda moseyed up next to her and leaned against the counter.

"Anything you need." She looked down at the older woman, who was a good five inches shorter than her five foot six. The nurse's dark hair mixed with gray pulled back in a bun gave her a grandmotherly feel. Maybe that was why, over the past year during which Staci had been visiting the hospital patients, Brenda had taken her under her wing, leading her to the ones that needed someone the most, so she trusted Brenda's choice. "You going to give me the story on this patient or are you sending me in blind?"

"Private First Class Phillips is having a hard time adjusting to his life now."

A buzz from one of the machines in the room across the hall had Brenda moving away from the counter. "He's the last room on the right, but don't be surprised if he's unwilling to talk to you. He's a grumpy cat."

"I'll see what I can do for him." She tucked a strand of hair behind her ear and headed toward the room Brenda pointed out. She tried not to remember how many times her mother had said those very words. *Dad's having a hard time adjusting to life. Don't worry and go play.* Maybe if she had worried, or if PTSD wasn't something to be ashamed of, things would have been different. Back then, PTSD wasn't something that was talked about; it was a deep dark secret kept hidden away in shame. Everyone tried to forget it.

From the doorway, she could only make out a figure in bed. With the curtains drawn and the only light shining coming from the hallway, it was hard to make out any details. She tapped on the door. "Private First Class Phillips?"

"Go away," he ordered without looking toward the door.

"I'm not a doctor, I have no medication, and I'm not here to question you or give you orders."

"Then what do you want?"

She took that as close to an invite as she was going to get and strolled toward the bed. "Just to talk. We can discuss whatever you want. I'm only here to visit."

"Unless you brought whiskey, I don't want a visitor and I don't need anyone's pity. I just want to be left alone."

"Do whiskey brown eyes count?" As she neared the bed, she realized the sheets fell flat where his left leg should have been.

That time he did turn and glare at her, but after a moment, a small smile spread across his face. "While I might be able to get lost in those eyes, I was talking about a bottle of whiskey. Now you didn't just stumble upon my room, so who sent you?"

"One of the nurses, Brenda, thought you could use someone to talk to.

Someone that isn't here to judge you or determine if you're fit for duty. Just a friend." She raised an eyebrow at the deep laugh that vibrated his whole body.

"Fit for duty…" His words trailed off as he tugged back the sheet so she could see the full extent of his injuries. "You must be crazy. I'm being medically discharged. Everything I've worked for tossed down the drain. I should have died."

"You were given a second chance at life, which means you're meant to do something amazing."

"Like this? What good is half a man?"

She pulled the cover back over him, not because she was disgusted by what she saw but to keep the burns and bandages protected. "You're still the man you were before. Just because you're injured doesn't make you less so. Physical therapy will help you learn to use the prosthetic leg. You'll be able to walk and drive again. You can do the same with the prosthetic arm, but most get to the point where they become comfortable without it."

"How do you know so much about this? From what I can see, you have all your limbs intact."

"I'm in my last semester to become a physical therapist. I've worked with many amputees over the years, some through rehab but most of them right here in this hospital. I'm not going to lie to you and tell you it's easy but you're a Marine, you don't give up. You'll push through in the end. You'll be stronger and you'll get your life back."

"That's easy for you to say; you're not the cripple."

"I think you need to consider the fact things could be worse. You still have one good arm and leg. Some who come back don't have that. You'll learn to do things with your other arm and you will move past this. You survived. So many others didn't." She tried not to sound harsh but she knew first-hand the cost of war. His reactions were natural but from the look of things and the fact he wasn't drugged up from the pain, it was obvious he'd been there for some time.

He needed a wakeup call because, with his burns healing, he'd be discharged from the hospital in a few days.

"I'd rather have been one of those who didn't make it back. I'd have changed places with Weber in a heartbeat if it meant he'd be able to come back to his wife and son."

"You believe you're half a man because of your injuries, but you'd want someone else to suffer them instead of you. Cruel, isn't that?"

"If it meant he'd be here with his family, then yes, I'd gladly change places with him. Half a man is better than dead."

"You're right there, and you should be thankful you're still alive." She stood, grabbed one of the small cards she carried, and held it out to him. "My name and number. If you want to talk, call me and I'll stop by." When he didn't take it, she placed it on the bedside table.

"I don't need your pity."

"Good because I don't pity you." When she reached the door she turned back to look at him one final time. "Think about what I said. You've been given a second chance at life. Don't waste it."

She forced herself to walk from his room and into the hallway. To see him with such sadness in his eyes tore at her heart. That look was the same one her father had when he returned to the ranch. Only her father hadn't lost any limbs; he'd had burns over half his body from an incident that had killed the rest of this team. She might have been harsh on Phillips, but if it kept him from doing what her father did, then that's all that mattered. He needed to accept things as they were so he could move on and begin to live again.

"Any luck with PFC Phillips?" Brenda stood just a few feet away making notes in a chart.

"Not really. He's angry, and like you said, he's having a hard time dealing with this. Has a therapist spoken with him? Someone with more training than I have?"

"He has more than enough medical staff pestering him. What he needs is a friend. The only one that's come to visit him is Gunnery Sergeant Diamond, his old platoon sergeant. Even then, he barely acknowledged him."

"I'm not feeling very well today, but I'll come back in a few days and try to talk to him again."

"You're not coming down with something, are you?"

"No, nothing like that. Just a headache. My neighbor had a big bash yesterday and it ran late into the night. So with the lack of sleep and everything, it's not helping. I think I better head home." She continued on her way down the hall before Brenda could question her further. It wasn't a complete lie; she did have a minor headache, but it was due more to the memories that refused to leave her alone than to her neighbor's party.

She grabbed her bag from the nurses' station and sped up her pace. For the first time since she'd started coming to the hospital, she was in a rush to leave. She needed to put some distance between her and the PFC. What she didn't understand was why the memories came flooding back to her now. It had been years ago when her father was in a similar position to PFC Phillips and even then, she'd been just a little girl. What did she know about what her father had actually gone through? All she had to give her any insight about him was an old leather-bound journal he had kept a daily log in.

The journal had been mostly filled with rants, but it was the emotions within the words that got her. So full of hate, passion, anger, and love. The words that filled the pages showed the battle her father had gone through. No one had tried to help him. Maybe she was just one person but she tried to do her best to save just one life—so she did what she set out to do. She used her own tragedy to do something good and stop another family from suffering further loss. If more people helped then maybe the veterans' suicide rate wouldn't be so high.

Dad, I'm sorry no one saved you, but I'm doing my part to save my generation.

Chapter Two

Two days had passed since whiskey girl came to visit and Kyle couldn't get her off his mind. Her sweet country girl accent played through his thoughts. She was the first one who hadn't tried to pussyfoot around. The heat and sadness in her eyes made it almost seem liked she cared, but why would she? She didn't even know him. His gaze fell to the card still sitting on the bedside table. He hadn't moved it because he wasn't sure what he wanted to do with it yet. He wasn't going to call her but it didn't seem right to pitch it, either.

With his burns healing and the infection under control, he'd be discharged the following day. Then he'd never see her again. That very idea sent a twinge of sadness through him. "Get a hold of yourself. What would she want with you? She was only here to show sympathy and support, not because she actually cared."

Why would anyone care when his girlfriend hadn't even bothered to come see him in person to break things off? After a little more than a year dating, he'd learned her true nature. One he should have seen before but chose to remain in denial of his suspicions. He'd cared for her and hadn't wanted to see that side of her. She was a flag chaser—a woman only with a service member because of the uniform—and now he had nothing to offer her. She'd gone on to her next target and he was alone.

While he should have been grateful that she had just left him be instead of stringing him along even further, he couldn't help but see her betrayal as yet another loss. *Another thing this war has taken from me.* He'd joined the Marines to make a better life for himself. It wasn't like he had anything else. As a ward of the state, he had been tossed to the curb at eighteen with little money in his pocket and nowhere to go. The Marines were his way out. A way to make a life for himself. Even now, he wasn't sure what he was going to do. He had lived in the barracks on base so he had no apartment to go to when he was discharged the following day. Instead, he would be transported to a hotel, where he'd stay for a few days. Then, he'd either transfer into the wounded warrior housing facility when a space freed up or he could find something on his own and put a request in for off base housing. For now, anything would be better than looking at these pale gray walls and the awful stench of illness and bleach that seemed to cling to the place.

They had pushed for a medical halfway home to help him, but he had refused. He had been fitted for his prosthesis, and physical therapy to learn to walk on it would begin soon. In the meantime, he was stuck in the wheelchair.

Nothing screams cripple like a fucking wheelchair.

At least, he'd be out of this place and he could get some whiskey. His mouth watered at the very thought of that earthy flavor, so full bodied that it burned its way to the gut.

"Knock, knock." The woman from the other day stood in the doorframe. Her blonde hair, full of golden highlights, looked windblown while at the same time making her more attractive. The jeans and light brown sweater gave her an innocent look. She couldn't have been more than twenty-one.

"You again?" The emotions that swirled within him were too numerous to count. He didn't want to see her but a small part of him was intrigued by her. What brought her to this hospital? She didn't work on base, wasn't military; she was just a volunteer. What did she know about the struggles the patients here were dealing with? Sure, she was nearly finished with her degree in physical therapy, but she could work with anyone. Why amputees?

"Mind if I come in?"

"Suit yourself." He fiddled with the edge of the sheet as she strolled toward him. She grabbed the only chair in the room and came to sit next to him.

"I hear you're being discharged tomorrow. I'll bet you're glad to leave this place." She crossed a leg over the others and he couldn't tear his gaze from it as she did.

"I'm going from one prison to another. I'll spend the next several days at a hotel until I find somewhere else and get my request for off base housing approved. Somewhere wheelchair accessible until I've learned to walk with my prosthesis. At least I'll be able to have some privacy instead of staff popping in every two minutes."

"There are always benefits to every situation if you only look." She tipped her head to the card that still sat on the bedside table. "I see you still have that. Please, take it with you and call me if you want to talk."

"There are others here that need your help. Why take pity on a lost cause?"

"You're not a lost cause. Actually, I think you have a lot of potential if you can get through this, and if you let me and the others help, you will." They sat there in silence for a long moment before she leaned forward. "So, Private First Class Phillips, tell me about yourself."

Private First Class. Would there ever come a time those words wouldn't send shooting pains through his chest and ice his veins? One damn moment changed everything.

"Private…"

"Kyle!" His voice rose but he couldn't help it. "Please, Kyle, just Kyle." He said it over and over again as if he could forget his title as a Marine and just be Kyle. To rewind to a few years earlier when he was but a kid, living life to the fullest—to just before he'd gone to the recruiter. Then, none of this would have happened.

"Okay, Kyle." She placed a hand on the bed, but didn't touch him. "Are you okay?"

"Fine." He took a deep breath and forced the memories away. "What do you want to know?"

"One of the nurses said you haven't had any visitors since you've been here, except your Gunnery Sergeant. Where's your family?"

"You go for the heart of things, don't you?" Not that he had any doubt about that. She had already proved she was feisty. "If we're going to do this, then we play by my rules. For every question you ask, you have to answer one about yourself. Deal?"

She paused and seemed to be considering it for a moment before she finally nodded. "This isn't how it normally works, but okay. My question still stands."

"I was a ward of the state until I turned eighteen. No parents or siblings. Even my best friend is…dead." He swallowed the lump in his throat at the very thought of Weber. "What about your family?"

"My mother's still in Kentucky where she's a veterinarian. She's unhappy that I'm not following in her footsteps. No siblings."

"What about your father?"

She raised an eyebrow at him. "I thought this was one question each. I'll answer it but it will cost you two. My father died years ago. Now, your turn. Why did you join the Marines?"

He pressed the button to raise the bed a little. No matter how much he tried, he couldn't get away from that topic. Just as the foster care was a part of his life, so were the Marines, and neither topic was one he wanted to discuss. "I aged out of the system and needed something. Joining the military seemed to be the best idea because it gave me everything I needed. As for the Marines, that just kind of happened. I went to the recruiting office and a Marine spoke to me. I signed up and shipped off to boot camp a week later."

"Since you just fell into the military, what did you grow up wanting to do?"

"Crazy as it sounds, I wanted to be an accountant. Something about numbers always drew me in. Math was the one class in school I excelled at. Everything else I goofed off and hated every moment of it." He thought back to his high school math teacher, who'd inspired him to do better. She told him he could do whatever he wanted if he only applied himself. "Why physical therapy?"

"It's a means to an end."

"Huh?" He wasn't sure what she meant.

"It's kind of a long story." She adjusted and scooted her chair closer to the bed. "When I was young I wanted to be a doctor. I wanted to help people, but I was raised on a horse ranch and I've always wanted to own one. There's a certain one I've had my eye on for years. When I sat down and really thought about it, I realized that dream was more important to me than being a doctor. This will get me there."

"A ranch—interesting. What made it more important?" He realized he'd asked a second question before she got to slip in hers.

"My father was a horse trainer and always wanted to own one but life had other plans. So I'm going to do it in his memory. But now, I get two questions. Why have you turned away those who have tried to help you?"

"Prying." He tugged the blankets up farther, trying to ease his discomfort. "I don't need help."

"Liar."

"That's not a question," he pointed out.

"You haven't answered my question honestly, so it still stands." She uncrossed her legs and leaned closer. "You've been through a lot. There's so much pain in your eyes but you refuse to talk to anyone. Why?"

"What I've seen isn't any worse than what others have witnessed or lived through. All they want to do is give me drugs. I don't want drugs that will make me forget, cloud my judgement, or act like a zombie. I'm learning to live with my ghosts."

"You don't want prescription drugs; instead you'd prefer whiskey. Alcohol will only help you forget for a little while. You'll need to talk about it to move forward."

"What do you know about it?"

"More than you think." She stood and moved away from the bed. "My father…his Army service changed him. Not just physically with his burns, but also mentally. He came home to us different. At first, he chose alcohol as a way to keep the memories at bay, but as the weeks passed he had to drink more and more to do the job. Eventually, it wasn't enough and he took other means to end the horrible thoughts…permanently."

"I'm sorry for your loss, but things are different for me."

"Isn't that what everyone thinks?"

She kept her back to him and, had it been months ago, before he'd ended up as a cripple, he'd have gone to her. Comforted her. Instead, he lay in that bed, useless, and it confirmed once again that he'd never be good enough. *Stop taking up space and resources that could help someone else. You're not worth it any longer.*

"I lost my father because no one helped him. Maybe he was like you and wouldn't let anyone in but Mom tried to shelter me from his *problems.* The only time I had any quality time with Dad was when she was on a vet call and we were on the ranch together, taking care of the horses. We bonded over that but I could tell something was wrong. It wasn't until my senior year in high school that I found his journals."

"Journals." It might have been sexist but he had always thought that was more of a woman thing.

"Yeah." She turned to glance at him. "Don't sound so surprised; a lot of men keep journals. It's also not uncommon for those in counseling to do it. Dad never went to see a counselor so I'm not sure why he started writing one.

Maybe it was because he did it with the horses. He kept a journal of their lives for the owners. Accomplishments, training, everything. He might have thought getting it down on paper would help. I'm not sure, but it left me with an insight about him that I never had before."

"So that's why you're here? You couldn't save your father, so now I'm what? A surrogate?"

She spun around on her heels to face him, her face alight with anger as she glared at him. "How dare you?"

"Hit a sore spot?" The pain in her eyes almost stopped him—she didn't deserve him lashing out at her—but the need to keep her off him proved too overpowering. "Well, I don't like being a replacement for someone you couldn't save. I've said it a thousand times before and I'll say it again: I'm fine. I don't need anyone's help, pity, or anything else."

"Fine. I know there's plenty of others here who would love the company." She nearly ran to the door, but paused before she passed through. "I wish you all the best. Don't let the people that care about you down because you don't like me. You can get through this." With that, she was gone.

Don't let people down…if only I hadn't already. If only I hadn't changed places with you, Weber, you'd still be alive. Crippled but alive to be with your wife and child.

Staci spent the next two hours visiting with those who actually wanted her company. Yet, even as she tried to make small talk with the ones she had come to know, her thoughts continued to wander back to PFC Phillips. He'd tried to hide it but the pain he felt inside dug deeper than she had imagined. No one could help him until he was ready, but even with that knowledge, she couldn't just sit on the sidelines and wait. Tomorrow, when he was discharged, he'd turn to the one thing her father had sought comfort from as well—alcohol. Even if he found solace in it, this would only be temporary. What the bottle led to would be worse, possibly even fatal. That wasn't something she could live with.

She wanted to wander back down the hall to his room to get him to see reason. It wouldn't be as easy as that. She could try as much as she wanted but until he could see what he was doing to himself and became aware he did still have a future, she might as well try to help a solid brick wall fall down with her bare hands.

You're only doing this because you couldn't save your father...

Maybe he was right. She had started to volunteer with service members because of the impact of her father's return from war and his suicide had on her life, but it wasn't what kept her going day after day. She continued to volunteer because of what she saw. She watched as those who'd seen unimaginable horrors came to terms with their grief and made their lives better. They didn't let the horrors they'd witnessed keep them down. Rather, they lived for the ones who would never make it back home to their families. They took joy from the little things. They'd watch the sunrise as if they'd never seen it before.

That's why she did what she did.

It didn't matter if someone was for or against the war. What mattered was, America was there for those who put everything on the line to stand up and fight for freedom. America is what it is because of those who are willing to fight for the land and the people's rights. She was only doing a small part to give back. *I'm not giving up on you, PFC Phillips. You're worth fighting for.*

Marissa Dobson

Born and raised in the Pittsburgh, Pennsylvania area, Marissa Dobson now resides about an hour from Washington, D.C. She's a lady who likes to keep busy, and is always busy doing something. With two different college degrees, she believes you're never done learning.

Being the first daughter to an avid reader, this gave her the advantage of learning to read at a young age. Since learning to read she has always had her nose in a book. It wasn't until she was a teenager that she started writing down the stories she came up with.

Marissa is blessed with a wonderful supportive husband, Thomas. He's her other half and allows her to stay home and pursue her writing. He puts up with all her quirks and listens to her brainstorm in the middle of the night.

Her writing buddy Pup Cameron, a cocker spaniel, is always around to listen to her bounce ideas off him. He might not be able to answer, but he's helpful in his own ways.

She loves to hear from readers so send her an email at marissa@marissadobson.com or visit her online at http://www.marissadobson.com.

OTHER BOOKS BY MARISSA DOBSON

Alaskan Tigers:

Tiger Time

The Tiger's Heart

Tigress for Two

Night with a Tiger

Trusting a Tiger

Alaskan Tigers Box Set Vol. 1

Jinx's Mate

Two for Protection

Bearing Secrets

Tiger Tracks

Healing the Clan

Alaskan Tigers Box Set Vol. 2

Her Black Tiger

Tiger Troubl

Alpha Claimed

Forever Creek Shifters:

Forever's Fight

Protecting Forever

Stormkin:

Storm Queen

Crimson Hollow:

Romancing the Fox

Loving the Bears

A Lion's Chance

Swift Move

Purrable Lion

Bearly Alive

Saved by a Lion

Furever Mated Box Set

Reaper:

A Touch of Death

SEALed for You:

Ace in the Hole

Explosive Passion

Operation Family

Marine for You:

Lucky Chance

Back from Hell

A Marine's Second Chance

United Homefront Ranch:

Destination Heaven

Tanner Cycles:

Until Sydney

Phantom Security:

Different Sides

Undercover Agent

Cedar Grove Medical:

Hope's Toy Chest

Destiny's Wish

Leena's Dream

Fate:

Snowy Fate

Sarah's Fate

Mason's Fate

As Fate Would Have It

Half Moon Harbor Resort:

Learning to Live

Learning What Love Is

Her Cowboy's Heart

Half Moon Harbor Resort Vol. 1

Beyond Monogamy:

Theirs to Treasure

Clearwater:

Winterbloom

Unexpected Forever

Losing to Win

Christmas Countdown

The Surrogate

Clearwater Romance Volume One

Small Town Doctor

Stand Alone:

Through Smoke

SEALed Rescue

SEALed in Texas

Starting Over

Secret Valentine

Restoring Love

www.ingramcontent.com/pod-product-compliance
Lightning Source LLC
Chambersburg PA
CBHW021002150626
46549CB00012BA/948